"It's too late now, Mother . . . I've already asked Gina to marry me."

Bitter tears scalded Gina's eyes. Without waiting for Mrs. Hamilton to speak, Gina wrenched the elaborate diamond ring from her finger and swept into the kitchen. Startled, Brent and his mother turned to confront Gina, their mouths forming speechless circles.

"You won't have to search for a pleasant way to retract your proposal, Brent," Gina said softly. With a metallic clink, she dropped the heavy ring onto the table before him. Brent stared at it with a growing realization. He looked up, seeking her eyes—eyes that blazed with anger and unshed tears.

"When I marry, it will be to someone who is man enough to leave his parents and cleave to me. A man who'll share my faith—not try to destroy it. A man who'll be one with me in mind, body, beliefs. When I marry, Brent, it will be to the right man—for all the right reasons. And because I know he is the man intended for me."

Gina glanced at Mrs. Hamilton whose face had paled.

"When I marry, it will be . . . *for love alone!*"

FOR
LOVE
ALONE

Susan C. Feldhake

BOOKS
of the Zondervan Publishing House
Grand Rapids, Michigan

Other Serenade Books by Susan C. Feldhake

Love's Sweet Promise

FOR LOVE ALONE
Copyright © 1983 by Susan C. Feldhake

Serenade Serenata is an imprint of Zondervan
Publishing House, 1415 Lake Drive, S.E.,
Grand Rapids, Michigan 49506

Library of Congress Cataloging in Publication Data

Feldhake, Susan C.
    For love alone.
      I. Title.
PS3556.E4575F6   1983   813'.54   83-6929
ISBN 0-310-46442-0

Edited by Anne Severance
Designed by Kim Koning

Printed in the United States of America

85 86 87 88 89 / 8 7 6 5 4 3 2

For my cherished husband, Steven, in honor of our shared love that rejoices in all God meant marriage to be.

months passed with time's good intentions failing to become reality.

CHAPTER 1

REGINA ROBERTS CHECKED the neatly folded garments in the suitcase opened across her bed and snapped the locks closed with a soft rasp. Gina hefted the bag to the hardwood floor of the room she occupied in her aunt's house and viewed it with dismay. Her luggage had never looked so old and shabby before! Deep scars in the brown leather bore mute witness to years of use.

When Gina packed for visits with her father and older brother, Luke, aboard the Roberts' family salvor ship, the *Sea Nymph*, the state of her luggage had been the least of her concerns. The aging luggage had been stored away in Aunt Nell's attic for over two years—ever since Gina had returned to Bridgeton following her father's death and burial at sea after a tragic diving accident.

Thirty-year-old Luke, six years Gina's senior, had taken over the salvor operation and continued to trek the ocean in search of sunken treasure. Frequently in the ensuing two years Luke had invited Gina to visit the *Sea Nymph*, but months passed with Gina's good intentions failing to become reality.

Gina whisked her fingers through the russet curls that complemented her topaz eyes and gave her a pixyish look when taken in conjunction with the light sprinkling of freckles dusting her nose. Gina sighed and hoisted the suitcases to carry them downstairs and place them by the front door. There she gave the bags a last critical look and recalled Maureen Lamkin's suggestion that Gina make use of Maureen's gorgeous, matching luggage.

"Take it, Gina," the tall brunette had urged. "I won't be needing it over the holidays." The slim fashion expert who was in charge of the Lamkin family business in the small Maine town was foregoing a Christmas holiday with family so her employees could enjoy the season with their loved ones. "You might as well use my luggage for your trip to Boston."

Gina had admired the rich fawn leather and was tempted, but declined the offer, deciding it was better not to be a borrower.

"Thanks—but no thanks. What I have is good enough for me."

Maureen's quick frown suggested that Gina's luggage might be good enough for her—but was it good enough for Brent's prestigious family? Quickly Gina had changed the subject.

Now, with Brent due to arrive within minutes, Gina wondered if she had made a mistake in not accepting Maureen's offer.

"It's too late to worry now. And . . . oh, what's the difference anyway?" Gina murmured.

To the young bookstore clerk, material possessions just weren't that important. Surely the Hamiltons wouldn't judge her by the condition of her suitcases. Anyway some world travelers considered it chic to use battered luggage that told a tale of travel.

The stately walnut grandfather clock in the living room—*parlor* as Aunt Nell insisted on calling it—bonged twelve times. Gina knew that Brent, who had a thing about promptness, would arrive at any instant. Hurriedly Gina fetched the shopping bag containing gifts for Brent's family and turned to survey the area to make sure she had everything she intended to bring with her.

At two minutes past noon, Brent pulled up in front of the house, halting with a squeal of brakes. Gina gave the tall clock a rueful glance, convinced the antique timepiece—and not Brent Hamilton—was off by a couple of minutes

The luxurious red sports car growled with a throaty rumble when Brent idled it at curbside and left the vehicle to hurry up the freshly shoveled sidewalk. Gina opened the front door before he had a chance to knock.

At the sight of Brent, Gina's heart quickened to a wild staccato rhythm that intensified when he brushed a kiss across her lips, then gave her a dazzling grin that made his amber eyes glow.

Brent was tall, well over six feet, with lean shoulders and a slim build. His brown hair, streaked by the sun, accentuated his burnished copper tan. The scent of Brent's musky expensive aftershave cologne filled the room and engulfed Gina's senses, making her momentarily dizzy.

"Ready to go, darling?"

Without waiting for a reply, Brent took Gina's coat from her hands and gave her a smile that mirrored his approval.

"As ready as I'll ever be," Gina admitted in a thin voice that failed to sound the chipper note she had intended.

Brent's dark brow slashed into a light scowl.

"I hope you plan to display more confidence than that when we're in Boston."

Although Brent's tone seemed almost bantering, his voice chilled by a degree and Gina felt chastised.

Woodenly she slipped an arm into the sleeve Brent held for her. He fingered the rich material and, as he snugged the coat into place at Gina's shoulders, touched the lush mink collar.

"Lovely coat."

"Thank you. I like it." Gina cast Brent a nervous smile, relieved to see that the shadow of doubt from the moment before had disappeared from his handsome features.

"Your other coat was fine for a small town like Bridgeton," Brent continued. "But this coat has . . . class!"

"It should for what I paid for it," Gina admitted with a soft groan. She glanced toward the oval mirror that hung at the end of the hall and smoothed her hair into place. "Maureen helped me pick it out."

Brent nodded with fresh understanding. "I should have known. Maureen has excellent taste."

Gina gave Brent a hasty look, then turned away before her eyes could betray the hurt she felt. Brent bent to pick up Gina's suitcases and led the way to his waiting car. She followed in his wake.

Gina knew that Maureen Lamkin had excellent taste in clothes. After all, that was Maureen's line of work. Besides the wealthy city girl had studied the field in some of the best fashion schools abroad. Brent made it sound as if . . . well . . . as if he thought Gina's taste was inferior.

Gina examined the hurtful thought as she waited for Brent to fit the items into the trunk. When he grinned at her and slammed the lid shut, Gina smiled in return and ordered herself to quit looking for hurts and insults where none were intended.

But Brent's careless words had pricked painfully. Helplessly her thoughts played back over various casual comments made in recent weeks.

No matter how hard Gina tried to rationalize away the

remarks of the past weeks, they stubbornly remained. She had no choice but to admit that there seemed to be some disturbing attitudes on Brent's part that had been over-shadowed in the excitement of planning the trip.

The way Brent raved about her new fur-trimmed coat marred the pleasure of the purchase. Had he been secretly ashamed of her durable, older coat?

The ugly thought clawed its way into her mind. As if looking to Brent for an answer, Gina gazed across the space separating them. Brent stared straight ahead, so intent on changing traffic lights that he didn't see or comprehend the look of puzzled assessment in Gina's eyes.

Was Brent ashamed of *her?* Ashamed enough to enlist the aid of Gina's best friend in Bridgeton? Was that why Maureen had insisted Gina buy one of the new coats the boutique marked on sale and why she had demanded that Gina accept a generous discount? Too, Maureen had casually mentioned, on more than one occasion, how differently people tended to do things in Boston. Was it so that Gina wouldn't ignorantly reveal her small-town ways for all the world—and Brent's relatives—to see?

The twenty-eight-year-old bank officer shifted gears and skillfully maneuvered his car through Bridgeton's noonday traffic, waving at several pedestrians as he flashed by. But Gina stared unseeingly ahead. Only with force could she wrest her thoughts away from the bothersome perceptions that had begun to plague her.

The couple breezed through town quickly. To Gina, the picturesque village was home. To Brent, it was a place of exile.

Like all the townspeople, Gina knew it was only a matter of time before Brent Hamilton moved away from the sleepy New England town. After gaining knowledge, experience, and on-the-job training, he would be prepared for a more prestigious position in the family's extensive banking system. Gina also knew that tongues were already wagging that when Brent did leave—Gina Roberts would go with him as his wife. With that idea in mind, Aunt Nell had spared no effort in impressing upon Gina the importance that her visit with the Hamiltons at their estate be a splendid success.

"Excited?" Brent questioned lazily when they reached the open road and he was able to maintain highway speeds. He gave Gina a sidelong glance and his mouth slanted into a generous grin.

Gina matched his smile. "Yes, I am. It's a beautiful day to travel. And the prospect of a two-week vacation is a welcome thought after keeping holiday hours at the store since Thanksgiving."

It was a perfect day—sunny; the air crisp and clear; the sky a deep indigo; and traffic was surprisingly light. Evergreen and hardwood forests along the highways were frosted with fluffy, pristine dollops of snow. Birds darted overhead, adding quick splashes of color. A doe turned to study the car as they passed by.

"The world looks Christmas-card perfect, doesn't it?" Gina mused.

Brent glanced about but wrinkled his nose at the wilderness scenery. He had a much deeper appreciation for bustling city streets and towering skyscrapers.

"It's okay," he agreed. "To me, it will be perfect to be back in Boston again." Brent smiled with anticipation. "After being exiled to . . ."

"I know: Small-Town-U.S.A.," Gina weakly interrupted to complete Brent's predictable phrase. "Where everyone knows everyone else."

"And don't forget, all their private business too!" Brent concluded with a long-suffering groan. Gina was so quiet Brent sent a worried glance in her direction. He noticed that she was staring silently out of the side window. "Now don't be insulted, Pet. You know I'm only teasing you. Bridgeton is a wonderful place to live—that is, if you happen to enjoy residing in the middle-of-nowhere." Brent breathed an easy, confident sigh. "You'll see what I mean soon enough, Gina. What's that old song? 'How-will-you-keep-them-down-on-the-farm-after-they've-seen-Paree'?"

Gina turned to confront him. "Really, Brent, it's not as if I've never ventured farther than the courthouse square! As a child I traveled a great deal with my family, you know!"

"I was only teasing." Brent's voice cooled another degree. "You will have to admit, though, you've hardly left the local area in recent years. You told me that yourself."

It was true. When Gina's mother died ten years before, after a long period of declining health, Luke had remained aboard the *Sea Nymph* with his father, while fourteen-year-old Gina went to live with her aging spinster aunt. Gina had rarely left Bridgeton since.

At the realization, Gina felt a pang of regret when she recalled Luke's Thanksgiving call and the eagerness in his voice when he'd invited her to spend Christmas aboard the *Sea Nymph*. She had hated to spoil Luke's impulsive plans, but was forced to admit she'd already made other arrangements. After the initial moment of stark disappointment that was easily transmitted over the ship-to-shore line, Luke's voice grew hearty once more, and he encouraged Gina to have a nice time in Boston. Gina sensed Luke had forced the cheerful tone for her sake. He missed her. Only recently had she realized how deeply she missed him, too.

"We'll get together another time," Luke assured her.

"Yes, some other time," Gina agreed quickly.

"*Soon*, Reggie! Do you realize how long it's been?"

"Much, much too long," she replied.

Before she hung up Gina promised herself—and Luke—

that she'd make a visit to the *Sea Nymph* just as soon as she could spare the time and afford the expense. Several times in the past weeks, a relaxing vacation aboard the salvor ship had held more appeal than the idea of a stressful meeting with Brent's illustrious family.

Enroute to Boston conversation became easy, and the dismal mood dissipated. Soon she found herself almost looking forward to their arrival. When rural landscapes gave way to metropolitan scenes, Gina knew they were not far from their destination.

"It won't be long now," Brent announced. "You'd better freshen up your make-up."

Obediently Gina snapped open her compact. She touched up her eyeshadow, decided her blusher was fine, and applied fresh lipstick. Frowning, she studied her reflection, hoping to pass Brent's inspection. Gina wanted to be at her best when he introduced her to his family—and especially his mother.

The thought of being presented to Clarissa Forbes Hamilton, one of Boston's leading ladies, was disconcerting. As socially correct as the ravishing Mrs. Hamilton was reputed to be, Gina hoped that Maureen's crash course in social customs would hold her in good stead. More than anything, Gina was trusting in God to guide her. She had faith that if she responded in a natural, sincere way to Brent's family, they would react in the same manner. Gina hoped that once they got past the first stiff, hesitant minutes that so often followed an introduction, the visit would be a pleasant one.

"This is it. Home!"

Brent swung off the wide boulevard. The snow-covered grounds of the estate were skirted by an awesome brick-and-wrought-iron wall that protected the extensive property as well as the Hamiltons' privacy. Carefully clipped shrubs,

14

iced with snow, snuggled against the foundation of the stately mansion. Strings of Christmas lights dangled from decorative cornices and were wrapped amidst ropes of bushy green garlands constructed of fresh evergreen branches. Gaily festooned gaslights stood like sentries guarding the entrance.

"What do you think, Gina?" The pride in Brent's voice revealed that he anticipated her answer.

"It's like something from a magazine."

Pleased, Brent nodded. "It's been featured many times —a real showplace. We're all proud of it."

"Justifiably so," Gina replied. "It's beautiful."

Brent took Gina's hand and led her to the front door. He stabbed the doorbell with a flourish, beaming down at Gina as they waited. Brent's confident attitude was infectious and Gina felt more buoyant and expectant than she had all day.

"Mister Brent!" The butler's dour face broke into an unrestrained, jovial grin when he opened the door and caught sight of the returning son, favoring Gina with a practiced smile before ushering them into the house.

As Aubrey turned to announce their arrival, Clarissa Hamilton swept regally into the room, a silk lounging gown floating behind her. Gracefully she moved to Brent, giving her son a radiant smile and a warm hug. Over his shoulder her eyes fastened on Gina, impaling the young woman with a steel-gray gaze.

"Son, it's so wonderful to have you home," Clarissa crooned and brushed his cheek with her lips.

With his arm around the petite woman, Brent turned to Gina. "Mother, I'd like you to meet my friend, Gina Roberts. Gina, my mother, Clarissa Forbes Hamilton."

"I'm so happy to meet you, Mrs. Hamilton," Gina said.

"A pleasure, my dear," Clarissa Hamilton purred.

15

Gina's distinct impression of the woman was that of a kitten with claws extended. A strained silence enveloped them, but Brent made quick conversation, with animated contributions from his mother. They chattered on and Gina trailed behind them, feeling very much the intruder.

Minutes later Brent's sisters, Gayle and Arlyce, returned from a last-minute shopping trip. Brent was helping Aubrey with the luggage, so Mrs. Hamilton made the introductions. Gina greeted the girls warmly. When Brent came back, Gina turned to speak to him, but not before she caught a significant look passing between the two girls. It seemed clear that Gina was exactly what they had expected—a disappointment! She was greatly relieved when Brent summoned her to follow a maid to her room where she could unpack and freshen up from the trip.

Alone in her room, Gina almost gave in to the feelings of despair that had engulfed her since the moment she stepped through the front door. If the situation didn't improve, how would she ever bear two weeks in such a strained environment? Wearily Gina sank to the bed and snapped open a suitcase. Her eyes were drawn to her Bible.

How would she bear it? Her spirits lifted. Through faith! Gina's eyes caressed the well-worn Book. She would live by the Word of God and follow her Christian principles. She would treat the Hamiltons with kindness—as she hoped they would treat her. And, if they didn't . . . she would turn the other cheek. For Brent's sake. For hers. But most of all, because that was what the Lord expected of her. Gina trusted that, if she lived and behaved in accord with her faith, the Hamiltons would come to love and trust her as Brent did.

Before Gina left her sumptuous quarters, she lovingly laid her hand on the black Bible and offered a prayer asking the Lord to be with her—in her thoughts, in her actions—and present to guide them all.

When Gina raised her bowed head, she didn't feel so alone. Things would work out, she comforted herself. With God's grace the visit would be the success she and Brent wanted it to be—if she was to share someday his love and his life, and take her place in the world as Mrs. Brent Hamilton.

CHAPTER 2

BRENT WAS AWAY, Gina discovered, when she descended the stairs after unpacking. Gayle and Arlyce, Aubrey informed her, were in their rooms wrapping gifts. Mrs. Hamilton was in her study returning calls.

Gina wandered through the house, following her nose to the cook's domain—the spacious, modern, gleaming kitchen that was a gourmet chef's dream come true.

Gina inhaled deeply as she paused in the doorway. The stolid cook gave her an inquiring glance.

"Everything smells simply delicious in here!" Gina whiffed appreciatively.

The round-faced cook nodded and presented Gina a quick, hesitant smile but said nothing as she continued to stir a bubbling mixture in a large kettle. The steam boiling up wreathed her ruddy features.

After receiving no encouragement in the kitchen, Gina retreated. She wished that Brent would come home, and crossed the large living room to peer toward the front gates. But there was no sign of Brent's approaching car.

Gina admired the lavish room where a huge natural pine exuded a pungent odor, bringing the outdoors inside. The room had been superbly decorated—probably by a floral service—with greenery, pine cones, red ribbons, candle arrangements, tinsel garlands, and other festive touches that lent the atmosphere of the Advent season. Neatly stacked birch logs in the fireplace awaited the touch of a match to kindling.

Passing through an alcove, Gina stepped into the family library. The book-lined room was vast and impressive. Gina randomly examined titles on the sturdy shelves but felt intimidated by the grim stares cast down from the oil portraits of generations of deceased banking Hamiltons. Gina turned her back on them and noticed the many unusual objets d' art strategically placed around the library.

"There you are, my love!"

Brent's voice so close behind her startled Gina. Alarmed, she whirled—directly into Brent's waiting arms. Laughing with delight he planted a solid kiss on her red lips. Brent's cheeks, chilled by the winter air, warmed in contact with Gina's smooth skin. He uttered a low growl of satisfaction as he pressed Gina's face closer to his.

"Did you miss me like a good girl?" Brent asked when she broke away.

"Terribly!" Gina's gaiety matched his own in the hope that Brent wouldn't detect just how very much she had missed him and how alone and vulnerable she had felt in his parents' home during his absence. Brent rubbed his chilly hands together.

"That's the kind of talk I like to hear! I hated to leave you alone so soon after we arrived, but I had a very important appointment to keep downtown." Brent's golden eyes grew mysterious. His deep voice dropped to a soft whisper as he couldn't resist offering Gina a tantalizing hint. "There was something I had to get for you that wasn't to be found in Bridgeton. This Christmas I wanted to get a very special gift for a very special lady."

Taking Gina's hand, Brent led her to the living room, handing his coat to Aubrey on the way. From a substantial collection of records in a cabinet, Brent selected an album of Christmas music, then lit a fire in the massive hearth.

With the traditional carols playing over the hidden speakers, and with Brent so happy and pleasant, Gina relaxed. Suddenly it seemed more like Christmas Eve to her than it had all day long. Gina felt a quick surge of contentment that engulfed her when Brent came to stand close behind her. He wrapped her in his arms and lightly rested his chin on the top of her head, while he hummed along with the carols.

"Just think, darling, our first Christmas together," Brent mused. Gripping Gina's shoulders, he turned her to face him. "It won't be our last," he promised fervently.

Brent's lips hovered over Gina's mouth before decisively dropping to taste her kisses. His lips explored hers with such growing force that Gina felt both thrilled and frightened by the intensity of his reactions and the feelings that his actions stirred in her.

"Brent! Someone might come in and see us!" Gina whispered as she pulled away and glanced nervously toward the doorway.

Brent drew her back into his embrace and chuckled. "So what? We're not children! I love you, Gina, and I don't care if the whole world knows it. In fact, I *want* everyone to know."

Even so, Brent seemed content to stroke her silky hair as they stared dreamily into the roaring fire. Gina's head was cradled comfortably against Brent's strong chest, and she could hear the steady beat of his heart.

Reluctantly Brent released Gina when the record ended

and the machine automatically shut off. Gina roused at the sound.

"Cookie is working her magic in the kitchen," Brent remarked as the aromas of baking ham and sweet potatoes wafted in to them. He checked his watch. "Dad will arrive home soon. We'd better dress for dinner."

Dusk fell while Gina slipped into a sophisticated emerald green dress and applied fresh make-up. The matching shoes Maureen had insisted she buy turned out to be the perfect touch. Gina was reassured when she caught her reflected image in the shiny glass of the French doors that exited onto the balcony.

Brent was waiting when Gina came down the stairs. Her breath caught under the hungry gaze he fixed on her.

"You're gorgeous. Utterly ravishing," Brent breathed huskily, obviously stunned. "Even Gayle and Arlyce will be envious when they see your dress." Brent cocked his head to study Gina with a look of pleasant mystification.

"Is something wrong?"

Brent shook his head and smiled slowly. "No . . . it's just that suddenly you hardly seem like the same girl. Somehow you look so . . . different. So very, very different."

"You seem different here too," Gina admitted her own uncertain feelings. Before she could proceed further with her thoughts, Brent shrugged, not bothering to search for any deeper meanings.

"It's the clothes. They make the man . . . and the woman, it would seem. The man I dress to be in Boston isn't the same guy I dress to be in Bridgeton." Together they stood by the bay window and watched the snow fall. The flakes, reflecting light from the fire, shimmered in the frigid air. Brent turned to stoke the dying embers with another log. It hissed and crackled as the flames licked

21

hungrily at the dry bark. Humming to himself, Brent stacked enough Christmas records on the turntable to last them through the evening meal.

Winston Hamilton had returned while Gina and Brent were dressing for dinner. When the elder Hamilton entered the room, Brent made the introductions. Winston Hamilton was a handsome, distinguished man, and Gina suspected that Brent, who strongly favored his father, would look much the same in thirty years.

"I'm so pleased to meet you, Regina," Winston Hamilton said. The firmness of his handshake and the sincerity of his voice made Gina feel genuinely welcomed by at least one member of the Hamilton family.

After a few minutes of conversation, they were summoned to the formal dining room. Heavy, ornate flatware and expensive china on the linen cloth reflected the golden glow from the slim white tapers in heavy candelabra. The flames dipped and swayed with the stirring air currents as the diners took their places at the long table.

With the help of a maid, Cookie brought in steaming platters of food, beautifully garnished, and began to serve. As was her custom, Gina bowed her head, clasped her hands in her lap, and gave silent thanks for the bounty before her. When she finished an instant later, she raised her eyes to meet the disdainful expression on the face of Clarissa Hamilton. From the corner of her eye, Gina caught Arlyce and Gayle exchanging meaningful glances. Although no one had uttered a sound, Gina somehow knew she had once more earned the family's disapproval.

Someone managed to pick up a thread of conversation after the awkward silence. Gina relaxed and enjoyed the remainder of the meal. When dinner was over, the family lingered with their coffee cups before deciding to have dessert later.

"Let's open the gifts right now!" Arlyce suggested impatiently.

Sophisticated Gayle gave her more impulsive younger sister a droll look. "I swear you haven't changed since you were a child."

"Don't act so high and mighty, Sis," Brent laughed. "If Arlyce hadn't made the suggestion—you would have!"

"Now, children . . ." Mrs. Hamilton warned in a merry voice.

Laughing, Win Hamilton took his wife's hand and led his family to the living room. The fire hissed when Brent took logs from the rack and gingerly placed them on the bed of red-hot coals. He flipped the stack of records, and music once again filled the air. Amidst the bantering chatter, and sounds of Christmas, the family members seated themselves around the tree, where a multitude of beautifully wrapped gifts spilled in every direction from beneath the sweeping boughs.

"How about fixing us something to drink, son?" Winston Hamilton suggested as he took his place in a comfortable easy chair.

"Good idea, Dad."

Brent crossed to the bar. With a flourish he mixed some drinks and Arlyce served her parents.

"What will you have, Gina?" Arlyce asked.

"Nothing, thank you."

"Come on! Join us for a drink," Brent insisted. He gave Gina a commanding glance before his eyes darted back to the row of liquor bottles. "What'll it be? A Vodka Sour? Tom Collins? Screwdriver? A glass of wine? Name your poison!"

Startled by Brent's manner and too shocked to speak, Gina stared. Brent knew she never drank liquor!

"I don't want anything, Brent," she replied when she finally found her voice.

23

Brent's smile stiffened and grew brittle. Gina sensed the eyes of the family swinging en masse to study her before moving to Brent, then back to focus on her. They waited, intent on her decision. Gina saw an angry, embarrassed flush creep upwards from the collar of Brent's shirt to recede into his hairline.

"Don't be priggish," Brent instructed in a low voice. He poured the amber liquid into a crystal glass with a gentle splash. "This will help you get in the Christmas spirit." His tone was now insistent, not to be denied.

"I don't need liquor to get the . . . the spirit."

Gina watched Brent's hazel eyes harden. "Just *one* drink, Gina. Come on, it won't hurt you!" Exasperation crept into his voice, accompanied by a spark of anger that flashed in his eyes.

Gina felt her own anger rising when Brent matter-of-factly approached her, drink in hand. Apparently he planned to put her on the spot in front of his whole family while they waited for a showdown.

What was wrong with Brent? He knew she didn't drink! He had accepted the fact before. Why did he feel compelled to make an issue of it now? Gina hadn't reproached the Hamiltons for their personal decisions. It upset her that Brent refused to allow her the freedom to abide by her own beliefs. Once again Gina felt that he was becoming a stranger—a man she had never known.

"I said I'd rather not," Gina whispered in a clear voice.

Brent ignored the statement and brusquely turned away after depositing the drink at her elbow on the end table.

"When in Rome do as the Romans, Gina. We're in Boston now—not straight-laced Bridgeton. You don't have to worry that someone will run tattling to Pastor Schimmerhorn if you have a drink or two. Feel free to live it up!"

Arlyce laughed. "Experience should tell you by now, dear brother, that those who live it up often have to live it down!"

"Enough of this. Let's open the gifts," Clarissa Hamilton suggested, taking control of the situation.

Gayle began distributing the gifts. Gina looked on as the Hamiltons opened their presents, while the stack of gifts beside her grew.

"You'd better start opening your packages, dear," Brent said, nodding toward the pile. "You'll be all night catching up to the rest of us."

"Your family will spoil me," Gina said with a smile.

Obediently she began opening her gifts: expensive perfume, a gold bracelet, linen handkerchiefs, a leather social engagement book, a silk scarf. Gina was touched. When she thanked the givers, they brushed aside her expression of gratitude.

Brent reached for Gina's present to him. Her heart quickened with expectation. Brent frowned thoughtfully as he shook and hefted the solid package.

"I wonder what this is—it's sure heavy!"

"Open it and find out," Gayle suggested.

Brent grinned at her. "Good idea!"

Brent sliced the transparent tape with his fingernail. Carefully he undid the silver ribbon and folded away the red and silver metallic wrapping paper to expose a sturdy navy blue box with gold gilt trim. Brent removed the lid to find a Bible, bound in rich Moroccan leather and lettered in gold.

At the sight of it, Gina felt the same rush of delight she had experienced when the book arrived at the bookstore the month before. It was the best Bible she could buy. The book was costly even at wholesale, as Gina had ordered it through her aunt's store.

When Gina had wrapped the Bible for Brent, she had

been confident he would admire and cherish her gift. She searched his face for some clue to his reaction. His smile was guarded when his eyes met hers.

Gina felt a twinge of disappointment that he hadn't examined the pages to note the large, legible printing on fine paper. Nor had he noticed that the Bible contained meticulous footnotes, maps, and a helpful concordance. Brent placed the Bible back in its protective box. Then his smile at Gina widened.

"Nice. Very nice! Thank you for such a thoughtful gift."

"Oh, Brent! I'm so glad you like it," said Gina, relieved.

Gina's satisfaction was short-lived as she realized that Brent was not going to pass the gift around for the others to admire. Instead he placed the Bible on the floor at his feet. A moment later when Gina looked again—it was gone—nudged out of sight beneath the dust ruffle of the sofa.

"Now the best for last," Brent announced.

He waited until he had everyone's attention before withdrawing a small package from the inner pocket of his suit. Gina had been so engrossed in watching as the rest of the family opened their packages that she'd all but forgotten she hadn't received a gift from Brent.

"For you, darling," Brent said.

Gina accepted the small box and plucked at the knot holding the elaborate bow. Finally it gave way beneath her fingers, and she slipped the filmy wrapping tissue back to reveal a dark blue velvet jeweler's box. Gina flicked at the gold clasp with her fingernail. Stubbornly it refused to open. Brent took it from her, clicked back the hasp, and drew the lid open to reveal a huge diamond solitaire in an unusual gold setting. The large oval stone gleamed with fiery, hot brilliance against the dark satin lining of the jewel case.

Gina stared at Brent. Her lips parted to speak, but no sound came. Brent smiled at her surprise. The tender, happy look in his amber eyes said all that needed to be said.

"Brent—I—I can't believe it."

Gina gazed at the ring as if she expected to blink her eyes, look again, and find it gone. In truth Gina knew how Brent felt; how she felt. She believed that someday she and Brent would marry. The meaning behind his whispered words that it was the first of many Christmases together hadn't been lost on her. Even so, the frightfully expensive ring caught her by surprise. She hadn't dreamed Brent would want to become engaged so soon.

"Well, Gina?" Brent questioned.

"Brent . . . I . . . don't know what to say."

Gina shook her head, dazed, unable to speak further. When she fully understood the awesome lifetime commitment Brent was asking of her, a thousand words, a thousand thoughts swirled through her mind. Without waiting for Gina's answer, assuming he knew her heart as well as her answer, Brent reached for her left hand and slipped the ring on Gina's finger.

"It's a perfect fit," Gina marveled as she held out her left hand to study the effect.

"Of course it is! I know everything about you—even your ring size. The most important thing I know is how much I love you."

"And I love you, Brent. Very very much!" Gina whispered.

In her eyes tears of joy shimmered as brilliantly as the diamond on her finger sparkled its savage beauty.

Gina's face was radiant when Brent tilted her lips to receive his kiss, and the Hamiltons clustered around to offer words of congratulations to Brent and to brush Gina's cheek politely.

"We'll be happy, darling, I promise you," Brent whispered much later when he and Gina parted for the night.

"Yes. We'll be happy," Gina vowed as she answered Brent's ardent kiss with a renewed desire of her own.

But *would* they be happy? Gina later worried when she was alone. *Could* they be happy? So much had happened so quickly that it was difficult to take it all in. It hardly seemed possible that only hours before she'd been in Bridgeton—in another world that now seemed a lifetime away.

Brent had changed in those few short hours. In some ways Gina felt as if she, too, had been changing and she was not sure she approved. She worried about the ease with which she sensed she could blend into Brent's world, leaving her own far behind. In Bridgeton her faith was a natural part of her everyday life. In Boston, under Brent's influence, faith seemed somehow antique and outmoded.

The ring on her finger was evidence that Brent needed her. Brent wanted Gina to share his love, his life, his world. In her heart Gina didn't know if she could or should exchange her world for the one he offered. Troubled images from the past months flooded her mind, erasing the momentary belief that she and Brent could share a happy future.

Why hadn't she noticed it before? Every time she had ventured to discuss something of a religious nature, Brent had always smoothly changed the subject! Now Gina wondered if she had been naïve to hope Brent would change because of her Christian influence and would come to love and cherish a faith as deep as her own.

Gina's heart was heavy as she pondered these dismal thoughts. A sigh escaped her lips. Never once had she questioned or pressured Brent to explain his beliefs. Never once had she mentioned his lack of church attendance.

Though she had said nothing to Brent about his apparent lack of faith, she had often prayed to the Lord about it, keeping firm her belief that Brent was the right man for her, that the Lord would transform his life, and that Brent Hamilton would open his heart to accept her Savior. Patiently she had waited for the prayers to be answered.

Now, alone in the guest room of the Hamilton mansion as Christmas Eve became Christmas Morn, Gina blinked back fresh tears. Not once had Gina given a thought to what God's final answer might be. Never before had she considered that God might already have answered her heartfelt prayers, and that His gentle answer was . . . *no!*

Gina's fingertips moved to her lips, still tender to the touch from the forcefulness of Brent's urgent kisses. When Brent had seen her to her room, he'd kissed her in such a way that it signaled he knew they wouldn't be apart much longer. The demanding, possessive touch of Brent's hands on her body thrilled her with promises of married love. She yearned to be able to yield to the natural desires for love's ultimate fulfillment.

How could she possibly feel all that she did for Brent Hamilton if he were not the right man for her? Before Gina closed her eyes in restless sleep, she prayed that if Brent were God's choice for her, she would be given that calm assurance. She must know beyond any doubt that she was following Him and not her foolish human heart.

CHAPTER 3

GINA TOSSED AND TURNED all night long. Many times she woke fleetingly, only to roll over and sink back into a distressing whirlpool of dreams. Many of the worrisome images that plagued Gina's waking thoughts returned to haunt her dreams. When Gina awakened shortly after dawn on Christmas morning, unable to sleep, she felt more tired and drained than when she had slipped between the satin sheets the night before.

Hoping to dispel her fatigue, Gina padded into the adjoining bath and took a quick shower before she dressed and went downstairs in search of Brent.

None of the Hamiltons had mentioned any plans to attend Christmas services and Gina had not thought to express her wish to Brent. Before drifting off to sleep on Christmas Eve, Gina promised herself she'd seek out a nearby church —alone if necessary—and celebrate the birth of Christ with other believers. Gina wanted Brent to go with her. She hoped—prayed—he would make the suggestion voluntarily. Gina's lovely face grew wistful at the thought. If only

Brent would freely make such an offer, she could view it as a flickering of hope that someday he would come to share her faith.

Hesitating at the base riser of the magnificent curving staircase, Gina recognized Brent's voice coming from the kitchen. Gina assumed Brent was chatting with Cookie as he relished a morning cup of freshly brewed coffee. Her footsteps quickened as Gina approached the kitchen.

"Good morn . . ." Gina's cheerful greeting died on her lips in a faint gasp. When she rounded the ivy-twined divider that sheltered the kitchen entrance, she discovered that Brent was not enjoying an early-morning visit with the Hamilton's plump cook. He was having coffee and an argument with a very agitated Clarissa Hamilton!

Gina's steps halted abruptly. Unsure of what to do, she stood motionless. Brent's low-pitched voice was calm but strained. When he spoke, it was in a tone so soft that Gina could scarcely make out what he had to say. In reply, Mrs. Hamilton's sharp voice was impatient. Her sarcastic tone revealed a distinct lack of good humor at the necessity of being up and around at such an early hour in order to have a few minutes of privacy with her eldest child.

Just as Gina considered entering the kitchen during a lull, another of Clarissa Hamilton's heated outbursts was punctuated by the angry staccato clicking of her high-heeled slippers on the glazed tile floor as she crossed the room to get the coffeepot for refills.

Mrs. Hamilton's shadow flashed across the threshold of the door, startling Gina. Instinctively the girl shrank back, suddenly wishing she were invisible. She held her breath and pressed against the ornate wooden divider until the decorative spindles bit cruelly into her back, her heart racing with a trip-hammer cadence.

Gina stole a nervous glance around her. Should she slip

away while she was still undetected? Should she make a noise—clear her throat, cough—in order to announce her arrival? Or should she wait a few more minutes and hope for a more opportune time to make her presence known? The decision seemed to be hers alone.

Gina stood rooted to the spot, helpless to move, as Mrs. Hamilton grumpily performed kitchen tasks and sharply lectured her son. Her subject was . . . Gina!

At the realization, Gina's heart momentarily stopped beating. For a long, horrified instant, Gina was so shaken she couldn't even draw in her breath. A wave of unbelieving dizziness swept over her. Automatically she clutched at the heavy divider to steady her trembling knees. Miserably Gina glanced toward the curving staircase. For decency's sake she knew she should leave Brent and his mother in privacy. But Gina was only human. She stayed to hear Clarissa's bitter, cutting comments. Numb, too hurt for tears, Gina had to strain to catch Brent's dogged, defensive replies.

"Oh, all right, Mother!" Brent finally burst out in anger that matched his mother's. "I will admit it! You're right—as always. Of course I know Gina's not our type!" Brent's voice was heavy with resignation. "But she will be when I get through with her!" A shadow danced across the opposite wall as Brent held up his hand and ticked off his plans, one by one, on his fingers. "I'll get Gina a classy wardrobe. Nothing but designer originals. The works. I'll pay to have a top hairdresser do a complete makeover on her. You and the girls can coach her with plenty of pointers. I'll give Gina a list of books she should read—although I trust she's already read most of them. Gina's a very intelligent girl." Brent's defeated voice grew chipper and confident as he spelled out his ideas. "With some work, Mother, Regina Roberts Hamilton will become the polished woman I intend to have for a wife—"

"A pipe dream, darling!" Clarissa Hamilton broke in with trilling impatience. "You can't make a silk purse out of a you-know-what. Don't be a fool! Why must you go searching for a . . . a facsimile when you can have the real thing. You need a wife from a good, socially prominent family—a family with connections as good and powerful as our own. Surely you went to school with any number of suitable young women."

"I did," Brent acknowledged. "But Gina Roberts is the woman I want. Gina's a gem of a girl, Mother."

Mrs. Hamilton dismissed the idea with a depreciating sniff. "A diamond-in-the-rough, perhaps," she conceded. "You're an idiot if you think you can transform a . . . social lump of coal into a flawless diamond . . . by exerting pressure. It may work that way in nature, Brent darling, but not in real life!"

"It's been done before." Brent's voice was hard and steely with determination.

Mrs. Hamilton's mocking laughter pierced the stillness. Her china cup softly clinked into place in its saucer.

"Really, you amuse me, Brent. I can scarcely picture you in the role of a patient Henry Higgins, toiling to teach your little street urchin to conduct herself like a true lady."

"Gina's a lady at heart, mother, and she always has been! She's good. She's decent. She's kind. She's gentle. She's . . . she's . . . she may be a bit, uh, unsophisticated by our standards, but . . ." Brent sputtered.

Clarissa Hamilton groaned. "Goodness, yes, I should say so! Gina's more than just a bit unsophisticated. And she's much too religious. Consider this, Brent Hamilton: A girl like Gina would offend many of our friends and business acquaintances. She'd probably insult people she met at cocktail parties, business dinners, or social luncheons. Those religious types make ordinary people very uncomfortable. They seem to manage to take all the fun out of a situation. You know how they are! Too pious to laugh at a joke. Too prim to take a drink. Too religious to . . ."

"Mother, I can handle that," Brent broke in with grim conviction.

"Can you?" Mrs. Hamilton's voice was scornfully doubtful.

"Sure! This religious jazz . . . it's just a stage Gina's going through," Brent offered in explanation. "A lot of people get all wrapped up in a spiritual experience for a while. Eventually they come back to their senses and get on with life. Gina's time will come. She's lived a sheltered life in a small town so that's all she really knows and understands. Once Gina gets away from Bridgeton and discovers there's a great big, exciting world waiting out here, I don't expect to have a whit of trouble with her *or* her religion."

"Good luck!" Mrs. Hamilton's chirpy comment was taut with sarcasm.

"Gina will make me a very good wife," Brent persisted. "So *you* may as well admit *that!*"

Mrs. Hamilton gave a huffy sniff. "I'll admit no such thing, Brent," she bristled, "because I don't believe it to be true. There are plenty of girls in Boston who'd be far more suitable for a young man of your background." Clarissa Hamilton paused and her voice softened before it cracked with deep emotion. "Why do you insist on being so stubborn, Brent? I wish you'd at least have confided in me before asking that woman to marry you! Maybe you can't see what you're doing—but I can! You're breaking my heart. Someday, son, you'll regret marrying with so little forethought. A girl with Gina's background—a woman from a family of beachcombers, scavengers, junkmen, or whatever it was you said they all do—will have a difficult time fitting into our world."

"Salvor work," Brent corrected patiently. "Professional treasure-hunting. It's a very respectable line of work."

Mrs. Hamilton wasn't about to be reasoned with. "Junk collecting," she insisted. "Anyway, if you're intent on marrying this girl—just to spite your mother—I suggest you waste no time in getting started with your transformation, my modern-day Henry Higgins!"

"I already have started," Brent replied smugly. "Maureen Lamkin has been a wonderful help.

"Really?! I'd never have guessed," Clarissa commented dryly.

"Mother!"

Mrs. Hamilton's voice lost its biting sarcasm and grew pleading. "Brent, darling, please listen to me. There's no shame in admitting a mistake. Everyone makes mistakes. This girl is your biggest blunder to date. Mark my words—beneath that sweet exterior beats the calculating heart of a gold digger. I know it! Forget what Gina says about having inherited a love for treasures and surprises. Don't pay any attention to the mindless reasons she gives you for that contesting, sweepstaking, or whatever it is she calls her silly hobby. Gina rattles on about the continuing hope that one day she'll win big, but it's just talk, Brent! Gina no longer has to chase after an elusive rainbow in search of a pot of gold. She's just found her pot of gold—*you!*"

"Mother . . ."

"Hear me out!" Mrs. Hamilton snapped, overriding Brent's objections. "Marry Gina and you'll live to regret it. We all will. I beg you—get rid of her!"

"It's too late now," Brent pointed out in a quiet voice. "I've given Gina an engagement ring. I've already asked her to marry me."

"Then *un*ask her!" Mrs. Hamilton's blunt suggestion was to the point.

A heavy silence lapsed between the two Hamiltons. Gina's heart thudded so loudly she was afraid it would betray her presence in the hallway. A rush of blood roared through her temples. The tense silence thundered in Gina's ears as she closed her eyes and waited for Brent to say something—*anything!* When he did not, Gina knew his silence meant at least a faltering of conviction—the beginning of agreement with his mother. When long minutes passed and Brent finally found words, his voice was a plaintive, faint sigh.

"You're right, Mother. But . . . how?"

Bitter tears scalded Gina's eyes. Without waiting for Mrs. Hamilton to speak, Gina wrenched the elaborate diamond ring from her finger and swept into the kitchen. Startled, Brent and his mother turned to confront Gina, their mouths forming speechless circles.

"You won't have to search for a pleasant way to retract your proposal, Brent," Gina said softly. With a metallic clink she dropped the heavy ring onto the table before him. Brent stared at it with a growing realization. He looked up seeking her eyes—eyes that blazed with anger and unshed tears. "When I marry, it will be to someone who is man enough to leave his parents and cleave to me. To a man who'll share my faith—not try to destroy it. To a man who'll be one with me in mind, body, beliefs. When I marry, Brent, it will be to the right man—for all the right reasons. And because I know he is the man intended for me. Chosen by God." Gina glanced at Mrs. Hamilton whose face had paled. "When I marry it will be . . . *for love alone!*"

Hurriedly, before she could burst into nervous tears, lose her resolve to end things quickly, or give Brent a chance to make a guilty token of protest, Gina informed the Hamiltons that she was leaving immediately.

"Just as soon as I can pack and call a taxi," she said firmly. "I'll get myself back to Bridgeton, Brent. There's no need for you to ruin your vacation with your family to see me safely home." Gina's words were calm with gentle logic. "You stay here with your people—and I'll return to mine."

Thirty minutes later the cabbie tooted his arrival. Gina hurried down the long walk without looking back. The cabbie came to her aid and Gina was grateful for a friendly, helping hand as she struggled with her bags.

On her orders the taxi driver took her to the bus depot and left the meter running while Gina checked her luggage and inquired about schedules. She still intended to fulfill her promise to attend a Christmas day church service.

"Could you be here to take me back to the bus station when services are over?" Gina asked the cabbie.

The short, round-faced man glanced at his watch and nodded. "Sure thing, ma'am," he promised. He touched the brim of his hat in a salute when Gina handed him a bill and told him to keep the change.

"Merry Christmas!" Gina said, smiling.

He matched her with a pleasant grin. "Merry Christmas to *you*, Miss!" he replied brightly.

Gina squared her shoulders, took a deep breath of the icy air, and hurried into the warm church where friendly worshipers were gathered to celebrate the birth of the Lord. The Savior of Mankind. The Heavenly Father Gina trusted to protect and guide her. The One Who had just shielded her from the human emotions that could have led her into marriage with the wrong man for all the wrong reasons. With the Lord guiding her, Gina remained free to wait for the man chosen for her.

Calm assurance, the feeling that Gina recognized as God-given comfort, filled her heart that day. The long bus ride back to Bridgeton afforded her the time to think and put everything into perspective. Gina understood that, despite the present hurt, what had happened was for the best. With the same strong faith, she trusted and believed that everything that had happened to her—and to Brent—would be used to fulfill God's purposes. With renewed fervor Gina prayed to do His will and be guided by His wisdom.

As dusk fell Gina stared out the bus window and reflected on the day. The scene with Brent was a painful memory. Mrs. Hamilton's ugly, untrue accusations had cut Gina to the core. But beyond Gina's heartache, disappointment, and grief, her spirits soared with rejoicing. Brent Hamilton was the wrong man for her. She realized that now, just as she also realized that somewhere there was the right man for her. The man the Lord intended for her mate. The man who was perfect for her in all ways. Someday, perhaps soon, Gina contented herself, this perfect man, this Christian love, would be revealed to her. But until then she would be patient.

CHAPTER 4

THE BUS DEPOT in Bridgeton was all but deserted when the driver parked the coach near the entrance. Shivering, Gina huddled beside the rumbling vehicle and waited to collect her luggage from the underbelly of the bus. When he snapped the compartment closed, Gina picked up her luggage and decided to walk the few blocks to Aunt Nell's home rather than take the time to summon a cab.

By the time Gina arrived on her street fifteen minutes later, she was out of breath. Her arms ached from the weight of her luggage. As tired as she was, it seemed an endless journey up the walk to the oasis of Aunt Nell's home. Gina didn't feel like sifting through the contents of her handbag in search of her house keys. Under the circumstances, knowing Aunt Nell didn't expect her back so soon, Gina suspected a key turning in the lock might badly frighten her aunt. Nell's bedroom light was still on, so Gina had no hesitation about using the buzzer. She pressed the button and a shrill noise pierced the twilight silence with an insistent drone.

"I'm coming!" Nell called from the hallway. "I'm coming! Hold your horses!"

The porch light flicked on to encircle Gina in a golden halo. Her face drawn, eyes squinted, Nell Roberts peered through a frosty upper pane in the window before she slipped the chain lock free. Aunt Nell tightened the belt of her blue chenille robe with a sharp tug before opening the door to her niece.

"What on earth are you doing back? Where's Brent? Has there been an accident? Regina—what's wrong?"

The questions burst from Nell with machine-gun rapidity.

"One question at a time," Gina requested, her voice edged with exhaustion, as she stepped into the warm house. She sighed, deposited her luggage on the braided rug, and sank into a nearby overstuffed chair. Then she unbuttoned her coat, unwound her scarf, and shook her russet hair free.

"Well?" Nell prompted. Her thin arms were folded primly across her chest.

"One—I came home because I wanted to. Two—Brent is in Boston with his family. Three—there was no accident. And, as for what's wrong—I suppose that all depends on whose point of view you're willing to accept, Aunt Nell."

Nell's brow dipped into a puzzled frown. Out of habit the aging woman fingered a few stray wisps of hair into the neat bun coiled at the nape of her neck, then sat down, perching on the edge of the sofa. She securely tucked her robe into place and idly plucked at the nappy material as she gave Gina a stern, silent gaze.

"You really haven't explained yourself, Regina," Nell rebuked in an accusing voice. "I'm assuming, however, that you didn't return to Bridgeton alone because things went so swimmingly in Boston."

Gina's smile was acknowledgment. "You get an A for insight, Aunt Nell," Gina murmured softly and glanced away from her aunt's baleful brown eyes. "Even though it was a disaster from the start, what happened in Boston was the best thing that could have happened."

Nell's deepening scowl told Gina that her aunt thought that utterance made no sense whatsoever.

"I do hope you intend to explain what is meant by *that!*"

"I don't know if I can."

"Try."

Gina remained silent. Aunt Nell wasn't her choice of a confidante. In the past when Gina had needed to unburden her heart, she had not found the woman to be always sympathetic or understanding.

"Maybe you'll feel a bit better if you talk about it," Nell coaxed.

"I don't feel badly," Gina corrected. "If anything, Nell, I'd have to say I feel . . . relieved."

Nell Roberts gave her niece a perturbed stare. "Relieved?" she echoed the word. "I dare say, I fail to understand why!"

"I'm relieved to learn exactly who Brent is. Who I am. Relieved that I found out what we both want from life before it's too late. You see, Aunt Nell, this morning I learned there were a lot of things about me Brent planned to change after we were married. I'm not guiltless on that count. There were a great many things about Brent I hoped would change too. Much as we seemed to have in common, it became clear in Boston it would never work. I guess, Nell, you could say Brent and I are two nice people who are not meant for each other. It's all over—and I'm relieved," Gina finished with quick finality.

"Regina!" Nell gasped. "Everyone in Bridgeton is assuming you'll be married. Now you say it's over? What will people say! Surely you're being emotional and melodramatic!" Nell suggested with hope. "Mark my words, in a day or two, you'll see it's just been a temporary mis-understanding. A squabble. A lovers' quarrel. You and Brent have come to know each other so well I just can't believe that . . ."

"Apparently we didn't know each other well enough."

Nell fell silent. Gina reluctantly explained the very painful situation that led her to discover she and Brent were striving toward unrelated goals in life and planned to live by conflicting sets of values.

"All these months Brent had planned that I would change, while I've been praying that Brent would become a different man. Knowing now how Brent feels—and how I feel—Nell, I could never marry him. Not now . . ."

"Brent asked you to marry him?" Nell cried, her voice both exultant and despairing.

Gina nodded. "He gave me a beautiful engagement ring last night. I returned it this morning."

Nell gave a sickly groan and slapped her forehead with the heel of her hand.

"Regina, you *didn't!*" she wailed. "You *shouldn't* have!" Nell chewed her lip and shook her head before she sought Gina's eyes. "I'm sure Brent doesn't want it all to end this way," Nell soothed. "After you've had time to calm down and sleep on it, Regina, you'll find out you don't either. You'll change your mind . . ."

"I won't be changing my mind." Gina's voice was firm.

Nell gave her niece a patient, pitying stare. "Regina, Regina . . ." she implored. "Don't be a simpleton! You can't be serious about letting a catch like Brent Hamilton slip through your fingers. Why, Brent's family is worth literally millions! It would be the same thing as being mar-ried to the bank itself. You'd be set for life!"

"That may be, Aunt Nell, but money's not everything."

Nell's laughter was a harsh, humorless outburst. Nell

draped her hand limply to her heart. "Please don't try to convince *me* of that idiocy, Gina."

Gina shrugged. "All right—I won't. The fact remains that I'd sooner be poor and happy than rich and miserable."

Nell's lips stiffened into a tight, grim smile. "You might just get your chance to find out how well you like being poor, Regina!" she warned lightly. "In case you haven't noticed, there aren't many eligible bachelors in this town. Especially socially prominent, well-to-do ones, who are interested in *you!*"

Gina stared across the room at the massive fireplace, then squeezed her eyes shut in the face of Nell's unreasonable anger. Gina fervently wished that her aunt would just drop the subject. From the mulish set of Aunt Nell's chin, however, Gina knew her aging relative had no intention of ceasing until she had used every argument in her arsenal.

"I'm not saying this to be unkind, Regina, but you should remember you didn't exactly have suitors stacked up on our doorstep before you met Brent. And, furthermore, Brent was intent on asking out Maureen Lamkin—not *you*—the day you met him in Maureen's boutique." Nell's brown eyes flashed, then narrowed. "So, if I were you, my dear, I'd make a point of swallowing my foolish pride and I'd make amends with Brent before some smart girl—like Maureen—steals him away. A man with Brent's looks, wealth, and social position won't come your way again. Don't be a fool by burning your bridges behind you!"

"Aunt Nell, please!" Gina snapped. "I've given this a great deal of thought and I'm not . . ."

But there was no stopping the opinionated spinster. Nell cut Gina off with a hasty barrage of words.

"Someday you'll regret this foolhardy action when you find yourself repenting at leisure."

"I don't think so," Gina calmly maintained her position.

"So what if Brent's mother hated you on sight?" Nell barged ahead. "For all the money the Hamiltons have, you can afford to put up with a little grief. Anyway, Clarissa Hamilton won't live forever!"

"Aunt Nell!" Gina was horrified by her aunt's mercenary attitude.

"Well, she won't!" Nell insisted defensively. "You're overwrought, and Brent is upset. You'll both see things differently in a day or two. My suggestion is to let Brent cool down. You can get him back, Regina. I know you can. You're a pretty girl. All you have to do is play your cards right . . ."

"All I'd have to do," Gina whispered in a voice that quaked with anger, "is throw away my convictions, beliefs, and upbringing. *All* I'd have to do is to conform to what Brent Hamilton expects of the woman who is his wife. *All* I'd have to do is ignore God's purpose for my life. Nell, can't you see I'd be selling myself by abandoning everything I believe in exchange for financial security? What kind of marriage would an arrangement like that be?"

Nell was unmoved and unimpressed by Gina's logic. "Most marriages are far from perfect," Nell pointed out. "At least those I've observed all these years. Most marriages end up as partnerships formed for one convenience or another. If love happens—fine! Well and good. The couple can count themselves among the lucky few. When love doesn't happen, smart couples make the best of a bad situation, keep their mouths shut, and make do with whatever benefits they do have."

"I couldn't settle for anything less than love. I'd sooner remain single all the days of my life than marry a man for the wrong reasons."

"Love, schmove!" Nell snorted and made a face. She

44

leaned toward Gina and her eyes became slits. "I'll tell you something about love, duckie!" Nell's voice was a hoarse whisper. "It's as easy to fall in love with a rich man as it is to love a poor man. A lot of girls—like Maureen—won't even date a fellow of modest means." Nell flicked her wrist in a gesture of careless dismissal. "Those girls are smart enough to know it's a waste of time to get involved with a poor man. If you knew what lay in store for you, Regina, and the hard future you're facing, you'd stop at nothing to get Brent back. You'd realize he can give you the world on a string—and wants to do it! Being able to accept all the Hamiltons could offer is worth a bit of sacrifice on your part." Nell paused a calculated moment, relishing the effect of her timing. "There's the telephone, Regina. Go call Brent. Tell him you're sorry."

"No!" Gina stood her ground. Anger thinned her voice. "Nell, I know you won't understand what I'm trying to say, and I know you won't agree with me, but I don't want the world Brent can give me—or its ways. I want something more precious than all the riches of Brent's world. I want the love of a good, Christian man, and a marriage I can treasure forever."

Nell rolled her eyes heavenward. "You're being a fool, and some smart girl is going to profit from your stupidity. And don't think for one moment that I haven't noticed the way Brent has looked at Maureen when they've been in the bookstore at the same time."

Gina knew Nell was craftily trying to arouse her competitive spirit, to fuel her jealousy. But the girl was past the point of desiring Brent just to keep another woman from having him.

"I have no doubt that Brent and Maureen could be very happy together," Gina said in a serene voice. "They come from the same background. They share many of the same friends. They have a lot of interests in common. I think they could make each other very happy."

"I don't understand you. Maybe I should quit trying!" Nell was aghast. "Most girls would want to scratch out the eyes of any girl who gave their fellow a second glance. You sound as if you'd be happy if Brent and Maureen got together."

Gina couldn't help the smile that flickered across her features. "I'm not most girls, Aunt Nell. And I don't hate Brent. I still consider him a friend—and I hope he views me in the same way. If Maureen should be the woman who can make Brent happy, then I'll be overjoyed for both of them."

Nell was about to speak further when the shrilling telephone silenced her. Nell glanced at her watch, then looked toward the jangling telephone in the kitchen. A satisfied grin spread slowly over her features. Her eyes glowed with triumph as she smugly regarded Gina.

"You may as well answer it, Regina," she instructed when it rang a second time. "None of my friends would dare call at such an hour. It's Brent . . ."

Gina hurried toward the telephone, fearful that Aunt Nell was right. Now that she'd settled the matter in her heart and in her mind, Gina didn't want to have to defend or explain her position again.

When Gina answered, a thin, hollow sound hummed in the wires. Then a telephone operator with an abrupt, unusual accent instructed the party on the other end to go ahead.

"Hello?" Gina repeated.

"Reggie! Reggie, is that you?" Luke's deep voice came through.

"Luke!" Gina cried with happy recognition. "Yes, it's me! Aunt Nell's up, too."

"Say . . . what are you doing home, Sis?" Luke asked,

perplexed. "I thought you were going to Boston. That you couldn't come visit me because of other plans. Did a New England blizzard blow in?"

"Nothing like that. I was in Boston, Luke. I just got back about an hour ago. I came back early." Gina paused. "Things weren't working out, so I came home."

"Didn't work out, huh?" Luke caught the special phrasing and correctly grasped the meaning.

"Right," Gina said with forced brightness. She shot Nell a glance.

Luke whistled low. "I see. It must be rough on you, hon. I can imagine you don't really feel like discussing it in front of Nell, right?"

Gina smiled at Luke's intuition. "Something like that," she admitted, relieved that he understood.

"Okay," Luke promised. "We won't talk about it now. Just remember to keep your chin up, your head together, and your faith strong. Don't let Aunt Nell get under your skin. I know how she can be."

"I'll remember that," Gina said. "By the way, how was your Christmas? Oh, Luke, I wish I were there! I'll bet you're having a wonderful time with your friend."

"No, my friend couldn't make it for the holidays, either," Luke said. "He contacted me last week to let me know something had come up, and he couldn't follow through with our plans. So, I'm alone with a skeleton crew of the guys who didn't go home to be with their families for the holidays."

"If I'd only known how things would turn out . . ." Gina paused, "believe me, Luke, I'd have been there."

There was a brief silence. "It's still not too late, Reggie," Luke pointed out. "I'd love for you to fly down right now."

"I'd like that too, Luke," Gina agreed. "But I can't

47

afford it now. I spent too much over the holidays." Once again Gina viewed with regret the money she'd withdrawn from savings to pay for new clothes and a host of gifts.

"Don't worry about that," Luke said easily. "I'll wire you the fare. You can consider it a Christmas gift from me."

Gina was tempted until she recalled how hard Luke worked, how costly salvor operations could be, especially when the expeditions were expensive failures. So many people already depended on Luke for their livelihood.

"Thanks, Luke," Gina refused. "I appreciate the offer, but I can't let you do it."

"You won't come?" Luke sounded as disappointed as Gina felt.

"Not right now," Gina softened her answer. "Perhaps in a few months. I promise I won't put it off much longer. I'll visit you just as soon as I can."

"Even if you won't let me send you some travel money, Reggie, I'll be sending off prayers for you. Things will work out, Reg. Trust the Lord, honey, because He'll never lead you wrong."

"I know. Thanks for calling. Thanks for everything, Luke. I'll be with you soon. Here's Aunt Nell."

Gina turned the telephone over to their aunt so she could speak with her nephew. A few minutes later Nell rang off.

"It's time to go to bed," Nell announced as she replaced the receiver in the cradle.

Gina nodded. "Don't worry about the store. I can go first thing in the morning." Gina said. "There will undoubtedly be a crowd of people bringing in books they received as gifts, have already read, and want to exchange."

"If you don't mind opening up, that would be nice," Nell said. "Perky will certainly be surprised to see you."

Mrs. Perkins would not be the only surprised citizen of

Bridgeton, Gina thought as she readied for bed. The whole town would be startled to see her home so soon, when it was common knowledge she had left to spend two weeks with the Hamiltons in their Boston home.

The news would spread like wildfire. By noon, Gina suspected, there wouldn't be a soul in Bridgeton who didn't know she was back—and *why!* Knowing that, Gina prayed for special strength and grace to help her cope with the pointed questions she knew her premature return would evoke.

CHAPTER 5

Just as predicted, Mrs. Perkins was surprised to find Gina behind the counter of the *Book Nook* on the following morning. Perky, a widow who worked mornings at the bookstore, was grateful for Gina's efficient help. Shortly after they opened the door to the public, customers flocked in to arrange exchanges. It was mid-morning before the two women could escape to the office for a cup of coffee and a chance to chat.

Although Mrs. Perkins had carefully avoided asking any probing questions about Gina's early return, she *was* curious and concerned. It was easy for Gina to unburden to kindly Martha Perkins, who had been alone since her husband's death five years before. Perky nodded understandingly at the dilemma Gina presented, and affirmed the decisions she had chosen to make. Perky understood because she shared Gina's faith.

When Gina finished her story, Perky silently sipped coffee from a large mug, thoughtfully reviewing the situation.

"A Christian marriage is forever," Perky offered her opinion. "Believe me, dear, forever could be a long, long time if you found yourself spending it married to the wrong man. Count your blessings—not the heartaches.''

A few minutes later the two women were forced to set aside their coffee cups and conversation in order to accommodate another stream of customers. Gina was relieved to notice that, after the first startled glances of recognition, the townspeople welcomed her warmly and managed to refrain from asking the painful, nosy questions which Gina had dreaded.

Maureen Lamkin arrived in a splash of color shortly before noon. Searching Maureen's face, Gina knew that the pretty brunette was already aware of why she was back in town. Maureen's green eyes were friendly and sympathetic.

''Maybe you and Brent will get things patched up.'' Maureen touched Gina's arm with a tender gesture. ''You're both nice people. I'm not going to take sides because I like you both.''

Gina gave Maureen a startled glance. ''I'd never dream of expecting you to take sides! This is no bitter feud. I simply realized that Brent is a nice guy—just not the man I want to spend the rest of my life with. I still care about him. I want only good things for Brent.''

''I'm glad you feel that way, but I'm not surprised,'' Maureen said. ''I don't think you have a spiteful bone in your body.''

''Or an ounce of food in my stomach,'' Gina admitted in a whisper. ''I skipped breakfast this morning because Aunt Nell's in such a snit over this.'' Maureen cocked an inquiring brow. ''I'm afraid Nell's taking it personally,'' Gina explained further. ''Somehow she feels I've let her down and ruined her plans.''

Maureen's long-lashed eyes grew somber. ''Oh, Gina! That's so sad. It's hard enough for you without Nell acting like . . .'' Maureen's voice trailed off.

51

"She'll get over it," Gina predicted optimistically.

Maureen nodded as she checked her wrist watch. "I haven't had lunch yet. Let's meet at the restaurant when you take your lunch break. My treat."

"It's a deal," Gina agreed.

"Terrific! And I promise, my friend, I won't even ask about your Christmas!"

Gina laughed. "I won't make the same vow. Incidentally, Maureen, how *was* your Christmas?"

Maureen tossed a grin over her shoulder as she strode to the door with long-legged strides. "I'll tell you all about it—over lunch—in an hour."

"Fair enough!"

A few minutes after noon Gina slipped on her coat, wrapped the wooly scarf Nell had made for her around her neck, and walked the two blocks to the small restaurant where she'd promised to meet Maureen. The tall fashion consultant was already waiting. Gina removed her outer garments and took a seat across the table from her friend.

Maureen reached into her handbag for a cigarette. "Oh! Before I forget . . ." Maureen extracted a bulging envelope from a pocket of her purse. "Here are proof-of-purchase seals, box tops, and other goodies I've saved for you to use with your contest entries."

"You're a doll," Gina said as she accepted the envelope. "Thanks! I just got another hobby newsletter last week. There are several sweepstakes I plan to enter. And some contests requiring original jingles. A few of the twenty-five-words-or-less endorsements looked interesting too." Gina tucked the items into her purse and closed the snap. "Some of the prizes are really super."

"Aren't they always?" Maureen teased.

"Not always the ones I win," Gina said ruefully.

"Don't worry, one of these times you'll win big," Maureen assured her. "I've read some of your jingles and endorsements, Gina, and they're really clever. With your talent, you can't lose. Just wait and see."

"I hope so. Anyway it's fun to dream. I do wish I could win something other than the consolation prizes though. I have enough caps, tennis balls, cook books, tape recorders, golf balls, knife sharpeners and small gadgets to open a store!"

"At least you've been winning," Maureen pointed out. "That makes it worth your time and postage. Someone has to win the big prizes, Gina. If you stick with it, maybe one of these days that someone will be you!"

"Now, tell me about your Christmas," Gina asked, changing the subject.

Maureen made a bored face. "Christmas away from family and home is just another day. Not that it was so bad," she amended quickly. "It's a fact of life that often the owners of businesses have to tailor their plans so employees can have the holidays off. I'll be taking a vacation before long."

"Have you decided just when you'll go? Or where?"

Maureen shook her head. "Not yet. I haven't had time to think that far ahead. I do know it will be soon. After holiday hours at the boutique since November—believe me—I can use a vacation."

Gina nodded her agreement. "Me, too. An overnight trip to Boston hardly constituted a getting-away-from-it-all-vacation," Gina sighed. "I wish now that I'd gone to see Luke instead."

"He'd have loved that."

"Luke called last night," Gina told her friend. "Last month he mentioned he'd invited someone to spend Christmas aboard the *Sea Nymph*. Knowing Luke would have a good friend with him made it easier to tell him I was going to Brent's.''

"It's nice Luke wasn't by himself.''

"But he was. I learned last night when he called that his friend couldn't make it, either. Something came up and forced him to cancel. After Aunt Nell began her harping at me, I wished more than ever that I was vacationing aboard the *Sea Nymph* in the Caribbean. I'm hoping I can afford to go before long.''

The waitress came to take their orders. When the food was served, the girls chatted as they ate lunch, then lingered over a second cup of coffee before they had to hurry back to their jobs.

Aunt Nell, who'd come in to relieve Gina on her noon hour, reached for her coat when she saw Gina at the door.

"I'll be leaving now, Regina,'' Nell said and tugged on her sensible galoshes. "I have some business to attend to. I expect things will be slow in the store until five when people get off work. If you need me—call.'' Nell stepped out the door and the bell overhead tinkled her departure.

Gina sighed, basking in the quiet warmth of the neatly arranged store. The streets thinned of people as workers rushed back to their jobs. No customers came in, so Gina decided to take the time to work on her contest entries. She extracted the newsletter tucked into a drawer with her three-by-five inch plain cards, envelopes, colored marking pens and scissors. Gina smoothed the folded newsletter flat on the desk and once again scanned entrance requirements, making neat check marks by those for which she was qualified and was interested in entering.

The afternoon passed slowly. Gina had to leave the back office and her contesting work only a few times in order to wait on customers. It was some time later when Gina glanced at the overhead clock and saw that it was going on

54

three o'clock. If she hurried she could have her entries ready to post with Tom Malloy, the mailman, when he made his rounds. It would spare her a walk to the post office.

Gina raced the clock and finished the entries just as Tom rounded the corner of the town square, his brown leather mail pouch slung from his shoulder. When he passed beneath the bay window, he glanced up at Gina and jauntily mounted the four steps into the bookstore. Tom's ruddy cheeks were chapped from the bitter wind. His glasses steamed when he entered the cozy building, so he shoved them onto his forehead.

"I didn't think you'd be here, Gina. I'm glad to see you are. I'll need your signature on this letter."

Gina looked puzzled. "My signature?" she asked.

Tom nodded and unzipped his coat, reaching into a pocket to produce a ball-point pen. He clicked it into readiness and handed Gina the form. Hurriedly she signed her name and Tom handed over the envelope.

"I wonder what it is," Gina mused as she accepted it and absently handed Tom the thick pile of stamped entries for him to post. When Gina's eyes focused on the ornate logo of the famous international cosmetics company, she gasped. Alarmed by the sound, Tom wheeled worriedly.

"Are you all right, Gina? It's not bad news, is it?"

Gina's hands trembled. For one long moment she didn't know if she were going to laugh or cry. She knew, without opening the envelope, that this win was bigger than all the rest.

"It's not bad news! Tom, it's going to be wonderful news. I know it!"

A grin spread over Tom's features, and he chuckled with anticipation. "Don't keep me in suspense, Gina. Hurry! Open it up and tell me what you've won."

At Tom's urging Gina slit the envelope and extracted the

crisp letterhead. Her smile widened when she scanned the contents. Impulsively Gina hugged Tom and held the letter so he could see for himself. In silence Tom read it, his lips moving, then he let out a delighted whoop. An elderly woman, plodding past the bookstore, twisted around to glance up through the bay window with a look of alarm.

"After all the entries I've posted for you, Gina Roberts," Tom said, "it's about time you won something big. Congratulations! Believe me, it couldn't have happened to a nicer girl. Wait'll I tell my wife!"

"I have something for you to tell Ginny. Tell her you're going to take her out for a night on the town—the best meal money can buy—my compliments. It's the least I can do, Tom. You've been so faithful about mailing my entries. I want you to share in the fun too."

"You don't have to do that," Tom said, although Gina could tell he was touched by the thought.

The bell above the door tinkled again. The pharmacist, Mr. Stanley, from the corner store came in. Before the druggist could utter a greeting, Tom blurted Gina's news.

"The grand prize, you say? Wow! What does that mean, Gina?"

"You tell him, Tom. I'm too excited to think or talk!"

Tom adjusted his glasses and read the list: a luxury Caribbean cruise for two, designer dresses, personalized luggage, five thousand dollars in cash, and cosmetics and perfumes from the sponsoring company.

"That's the best news I've heard all day," Mr. Stanley said. "It makes quite a Christmas, hmm, Gina?"

Tom departed on his rounds and Gina waited on the druggist. Before he left the bookstore, Maureen came bursting in, coatless, despite the frigid weather. She threw her arms around Gina's neck and hugged her in wild excitement as she congratulated and questioned her at the same time.

56

"I'm so happy for you!" Maureen bubbled.

Gina returned her friend's warm hug. "Don't be happy for just me, Maureen. Be happy for *us!* You, my dear, supportive friend, who stood by my contesting hobby through thick and thin, snipping and clipping, are going with me!"

Maureen faltered in surprise. Her mouth opened and moved but words weren't immediately forthcoming.

"You can't mean it . . ." The tall brunette was dazed.

"I do mean it! We need to get away. It's a trip for two and there's no one I'd rather take with me. And no one who deserves it more, Maureen."

A minute or two after Maureen had raced back to her boutique down the street, the telephone began to ring. Each time, Gina accepted the curious well-wishers' astonished words of congratulations, and quickly outlined the details.

"Yes, Perky," Gina murmured when yet another call came in. "What you've heard is true—all of it."

"It's a miracle," Perky decided. "An answered prayer. You needed to get away and now you'll be able to. You can even afford to go see Luke after the cruise ends."

"Perky, how fantastic! I hadn't even thought of that yet. I will! What a wonderful idea. But . . ." Gina's voice faded when the reality of her obligations dimmed the sudden bright thought.

"But what?" Perky nudged.

"I'm not sure I should plan to be away for so long," Gina admitted. "Aunt Nell might . . ."

"You leave Nell Roberts to me," Perky broke in, her voice firm. "And don't worry about the store. I'll be there any time Nell needs me. I know a few people who'd be tickled to supplement their income by working a few hours a day to help out while you're away."

Gina hadn't been off the telephone for very long when

Nell marched into the store. She gave Gina a long, measured look—a mixture of dismay and odd respect.

"You could've bowled me over with a feather when I heard the news. All these years I've thought your hobby was pure stuff-and-rubbish nonsense." Nell tugged off her mittens. "How soon will you be leaving?"

"In about a month," Gina said. "I'll be spending a few days in New York City collecting my prizes. Then we'll sail."

"Very well. I'll make plans for you to be away."

Gina was relieved when by late afternoon the initial excitement had died down, and people had ceased calling to question her about her prizes and plans. That night Gina offered a special prayer of thanksgiving. Deep in her heart, Gina believed as Perky did. It wasn't just a lucky win. It was a miracle!

Brent came into the bookstore as soon as he returned to Bridgeton. After an awkward moment, the two began chatting as old friends do.

"I'm proud of you," Brent said. "That's quite a coup. Maureen's been telling me you have a true knack for creating product slogans and jingles."

"I enjoy it. Sometimes I've had to wrack my brain over entries. This one win makes all the work worthwhile. I'm looking forward to the cruise."

"So is Maureen," Brent said. "It's sweet of you to take her along."

Gina smiled. "Maureen deserves to go, and I'll enjoy the trip more having my best girl friend along."

Brent and Gina talked awhile longer, although neither of them mentioned the memories of deep hurt from their brief time in Boston. Gina was relieved to find that she felt comfortable with Brent, even as she understood Brent Hamilton could never be more to her than a casual friend.

Even so, in the following two weeks, when Maureen and Brent began to keep steady company, idle gossips in the small town found it an interesting topic of conversation. Gina grew eager to get away from the area and the pitying glances of people who incorrectly assumed that her best friend had stolen Gina Roberts' boyfriend!

Impatiently she began marking off the days until Brent would drive the two girls to the train station. From there they would travel to New York City. While Gina arranged to collect her prizes, Maureen planned to visit some old acquaintances from college. Then they would be free to embark on their exciting adventure. Gina's heart soared at the thought of days and nights spent in exotic, unfamiliar places.

Before Gina departed Nell issued a brusque, almost un-friendly, farewell. Ever since Nell had learned Gina's full plans, the elderly woman had made no bones about the fact that she considered Gina a bigger fool than she'd first be-lieved. How could Gina possibly befriend the very woman —Maureen Lamkin—who was now dating her old boy-friend. The fact that Maureen was Gina's best friend and had unfailingly supported Gina's contest endeavors was lost on the bookstore owner.

"You're sure you can get along without me?" Gina asked one last time. A niggling worry crept into Gina's thoughts that Nell's irate attitude might be over the fact that she was leaving—not what had taken place with Brent.

In answer, Nell gave Gina a long look. "I've gotten along without you in the past. I'm quite capable of getting along without you now."

In past weeks Nell's grim attitude had been unrelenting. Gina was relieved when her aunt didn't accept the dutiful invitation Gina extended her to accompany them to the depot. As jovial as was the small cluster of townspeople who had gathered on the splintery platform, Nell would have cast a pall over the entire group.

"Here it comes!" Maureen shrieked.

Like a silver streak, a short passenger train hurtled around the long curve approaching the quaint town. Throatily the train bellowed at the crossroads and catapulted along the straightaway before slowing to a stop, airbrakes huffing. The train's wheels ground to a halt as steel clashed against steel. The diesel engine thrummed with low, restrained power, and a uniformed conductor hopped from the train to position a squatty stool on the planked platform.

"This is it, girls!" Brent said.

Brent gave Gina a friendly peck on the cheek and squeezed her hand as he wished her well, then pulled Maureen into his arms for a sound kiss. Friends crowded around with hugs, pats on the shoulder, and last-minute farewells. A camera clicked. The town's weekly newspaper reporter clambered onto a bench to perch precariously for a candid shot as the girls stepped onto the train. They turned, smiling and waving, as he snapped a final picture.

The conductor hustled them ahead, picked up his stool, and cried, "Allll abooooard!"

Maureen ducked into the train, laughing. "Do you realize we just created front-page news for the week?" she teased.

The coach was almost deserted. Gina and Maureen took their seats, but leaned forward to wave to their friends collected below. An instant later the train jolted, then gained momentum, moving faster and faster across the countryside and away from the sleepy New England town.

"We're off!" Maureen announced happily. "You'd better catch your breath now, Gina. You might not get another chance!"

Gina sank against the soft cushions and stared at the

wintry landscape. A contented smile tugged at her lips and her heart lifted light and free.

So much had happened. So very much. And in such a short while. It was the miracle Perky claimed it to be. In her heart Gina knew it. For a brief moment, she closed her eyes in a prayer of gratitude for the promise of the future.

CHAPTER 6

THREE WHIRLWIND DAYS later all the details were settled. With the prizes in her possession and anticipation in her heart, Gina approached the waiting ocean liner, the *Tropical Star*. Maureen's emerald green eyes sparkled, and she gave Gina a carefree smile as the girls walked expectantly toward the cruise ship.

The pristine white luxury ship, its prow soaring gracefully above the rippling water that lapped against the pier, was a magnificent craft. The stately ship was moored snugly in its berth, the gangplank secured for passengers to cross from the reality of the everyday into a dream world.

A seasoned traveler, Maureen was quickly drawn into the carnival-like atmosphere. For Gina, however, it was a new experience—far different from sailing aboard the Roberts' working ship, the *Sea Nymph*.

The girls threaded a path through the teeming crowds as burly dock workers yelled instructions to each other. Gina drank in the sights, sounds, and pungent smells of the harbor before she glanced back for a last look at the jutting skyscrapers etched against the horizon.

Both Maureen and Gina were too absorbed in the moment to break the spell with conversation. Maureen halted for only a few seconds, making quick promises to look up the friends and acquaintances she had recognized in the crowd, as Gina assessed the passengers who surrounded them. All the travelers were obviously wealthy and seemed to take for granted the luxurious accommodations. Their blasé attitude was in sharp contrast to Gina's reaction of awe and disbelief that she should find herself in such surroundings.

Breaking their reverie, a uniformed steward showed the girls to their quarters.

"Heaven, huh?" Maureen asked, looking to Gina for confirmation.

The stateroom was not only elegant, it was built for comfort. The cosmetics company had arranged for fruits and bon voyage party foods to be delivered to the room, adding an air of festivity.

"Do you mind if I run along for a few minutes?" Maureen asked, as Gina began to unpack. "I've seen so many old friends—I'd like a chance to look some of them up."

"Go ahead," Gina nodded with a smile and continued to unpack. "Just because we came on this cruise together, Maureen, doesn't mean we have to be inseparable. We can do that back in Bridgeton when there aren't new people to meet. So go have fun!"

Maureen grinned. "Did you notice some of the good-looking guys? Maybe you'll meet Mr. Right on this cruise, Gina! It's happened before." She sighed contentedly. "There's something so romantic about a cruise. Something that seems to put everyone in the mood for love."

Gina considered the idea that Maureen might be interested in trying her hand at the old art of matchmaking.

"Maybe I will," Gina acknowledged. "But, if I do, it won't be because I went searching for him. All I want to do in the next two weeks is rest, soak up the sun, swim . . ."

"And don't forget—eat!" Maureen prompted, and rolled her eyes as she patted her trim waist. "The food on liners is terrific. Not for the waistline, unfortunately. The cooks put luscious food in front of you every time they get a chance. It takes someone with will power stronger than mine to resist!"

"I'm beaten before we even start then," Gina admitted with a laugh.

"Me, too!" Maureen groaned. "See you later!"

The stateroom was a cheery place. The furnishings were comfortable and elegant, and the room afforded a spectacular view of the sea. The sleeping arrangements were cozy; the sitting room, unexpectedly spacious and inviting; and the large bathroom with a double vanity, shower, and bath would give the girls all the comforts of home.

When Gina finished hanging her clothes in the closet, she realized a bit poignantly how quiet it was in her stateroom. Noisy bon voyage celebrations were in progress throughout the ship, and music and laughter punctuated the low hum of conversation. A stab of disappointment pierced her that she and Maureen had had no friends to see them off.

While nearby partying passengers stole a few more minutes with friends and family, Gina looked out the porthole. Minutes later the vessel's horn blasted, its thunderous tone cleaving the air, a signal to guests that the *Tropical Star* was about to depart for destinations in southern ports. Guests at the bon voyage parties streamed from staterooms, pausing only long enough for additional hugs, kisses, and shrill reminders.

"Don't forget to send me a post card!"

"Take lots of pictures!"

"Have a wonderful time!"

"Be careful of the water you drink."

"Watch out for sunburn."

"Don't do anything I wouldn't do—but if you do—tell me all about it!"

After one long blast to rout stragglers from the ship, crew members prepared to set sail. Gina strolled from her room and was quickly engulfed in a crush of passengers who thronged to the upper deck and jockeyed for positions at the rail as the gangplank was raised.

Colorful confetti cascaded in the air. The ship reversed its engines, and the deck underfoot vibrated with the powerful rhythm. Departing passengers cried hurried farewells and hurled balls of crepe paper to friends on the pier, while those below leaped up to grasp the slim streamers that whipped and snapped in the light breeze.

Gina was wedged against the rail so tightly she could scarcely draw breath. Twisting, she searched the crowd for a glimpse of Maureen. It was useless. Gina was hemmed in on all sides by eager passengers. Those beside her were vying for more space at the rail. Gina had no paper streamer so she tried to maneuver herself away to give someone else her slot.

Her attempt was terminated abruptly by the jarring impact of Gina's petite frame against a lean, rugged, masculine form. Startled, she raised her eyes up, up, to gaze into the turquoise blue stare of a tall, raven-haired man. His penetrating gaze sent a self-conscious flush to Gina's cheeks.

"Excuse me," she murmured.

Without daring to cast the tall man another glance, Gina sucked in her breath and tried to ease past. Instead, she found herself firmly propelled into the very space she'd just vacated! She crooked her head around, puzzled and indignant. Before Gina could speak, a curled streamer was pressed into her hand. She looked at it uncomprehendingly.

"Hurry up! Throw it!" commanded the towering

stranger. A faint trace of impatience colored his tone.

Gina stared at him, managed a hesitant, uncertain smile, then did as she was told and hurled the brilliant blue streamer toward the sea of strangers below. Gina was oblivious to their cries of delight as they struggled to grab the banner. All Gina remembered was the haunting image of the most handsome man she'd ever seen in her life, an impression that would remain forever branded in her memory. As Gina closed her eyes, his image grew sharper.

The man was tall. Very tall. His shoulders were pleasantly broad, although his build was lean with the restrained strength of a coiled spring. From the quick but comprehensive glance Gina had given him, she knew he wore his expensive clothes well. The man's face was tan—but he had the burnished look of a man like Brent, whose skin darkened on tennis courts, golf courses, and the sun decks of cruise ships—not from laboring in the hot sun.

Broken streamers crackled and flitted in the crisp air. The soft noises snapped Gina back from her wandering thoughts. As the passengers filed away from the railing, Gina turned to follow suit, hoping to catch sight of the handsome stranger.

Gina expected him to have disappeared into the crowd, with only the intoxicating scent of his expensive cologne lingering in the air to remind her that he had ever existed. Instead, when she turned around he was there—having taken a step backward in anticipation of another collision. Had he been waiting for her? What a ridiculous idea! Yet when Gina looked up into his arresting blue eyes, she realized that that was precisely what he was doing, and her heart pounded wildly at the pleasant prospect. The man remained silent, seeming to expect—to *dare*—her to say something! Gina finally murmured the first thoughts that came to her mind.

"By the way, thanks for giving me your streamer. It was nice of you!"

The man's quick smile was cool. From the peculiar look that flickered across his face, Gina sensed that her remark had somehow disappointed him.

"It was nothing," he dismissed the idea curtly.

With sad recognition Gina decided that the handsome man at her side would have done the same for any stranger. He had not been attracted to her as she had been instantly drawn to him. His actions had been a polite gesture—the gentlemanly thing to do. No more. No less.

The striking man, who seemed to be in his early thirties, said nothing as he fell in step with Gina. When she didn't speak, his frown intensified.

Why did he expect her to initiate the conversation? Gina wondered. Why was he so watchful of every move she made? An uncomfortable silence stretched between them. Gina murmured a few words just to ease the tension.

Finally, feeling that further attempts at communication were inane, Gina gave the man what she hoped would pass for a carefree smile, made her excuses, and abruptly turned for her quarters. Just as quickly she found herself whirled about by an almost painful grip around her wrist.

"Come on," he said in a hoarse, impatient voice. "You aren't fooling me . . ."

At the mocking light in his eyes, Gina sputtered with shock and indignation. She tried to yank her wrist free, but he held her fast.

"What on earth do you think you're doing?" Gina gasped in a voice that was quickly rising from indignation to outrage. The man gave her a quizzical look. He broke his grip on her wrist a mere fraction of a second before Gina was forced to decide how best to ask the stranger to take his hand off her. He frowned at her, his eyes mirroring questions that she could not comprehend, let alone hope to answer.

"Come on, quit playing games," he suggested, lowering his voice. "Don't you remember me? Surely you must! I know we've met—I just don't remember where. I've been waiting for you to refresh my memory."

"I'm sorry. You're mistaken," Gina said in a level voice. "We've never met."

"Never met? That's impossible!"

"We've never met," Gina repeated firmly. "If we had . . ." Gina bit off the rest of her words before she could give voice to her thoughts.

The handsome man thought they were old friends, or, at least had once been acquainted, but Gina knew it was not true. Had they met before, Gina knew she would never, *never* have forgotten the moment.

At her words his glowering scowl intensified. He regarded Gina with an attitude that suggested he thought she was lying, but that he had decided to bide his time.

"I'd have sworn we knew each other from somewhere," he shrugged. "But—if you say we haven't—then perhaps I was wrong." He gave her a crisp smile as if to say that he would play along with her little game—if she preferred to deny the fact. "We can start with a fresh introduction. My name is Jordan Gentry of Gentry Enterprises. And your name, Mysterious Stranger?"

"Gina. Gina Roberts. From Bridgeton, Maine."

Gina saw the cogs turning in his mind as Jordan sifted the facts she'd given him, trying to mesh a connection, but failing. Jordan favored Gina with a lazy smile that took her in from head to toe, and his indigo eyes indicated that he liked what he saw.

"Your name is as beautiful as the woman who wears it."

"Thank you," Gina replied, even though she suspected it

was a standard line that had been used by Jordan Gentry many times before.

At his suggestion Gina allowed herself to be led to the deck of the ship where there were several lounges, game rooms, and other sources of entertainment. Her mind thrashed about for a plausible excuse to leave Jordan's side. When she found none, Gina suddenly realized that there remained no need to escape. Following the first few minutes when he'd frightened her with his aggressiveness, Jordan had been a perfect gentleman, and the conversation that followed was easy and interesting; his company, enjoyable.

"Let me buy you something to drink before we have to think about dressing for dinner."

"Something cool would be wonderful," Gina admitted as Jordan guided her into a small, intimate lounge where the bartender polished glasses.

Seated at a small table, Jordan signaled the waiter. Without asking Gina's wishes, Jordan ordered two mixed drinks. Gina's heart leaped to her throat and stuck there, making the words she forced out sound a breathy squeak.

"I'm sorry, Jordan, I should have told you. But I don't drink—alcoholic beverages, that is."

Gina glanced away from Jordan's startled expression to seek refuge in the eyes of the pleasant waiter who recited their list of soft drinks.

"Fruit juice would be nice," Gina decided.

The waiter accepted her order with a nod, then looked to Jordan to reconfirm his earlier order. When the waiter brought the beverages, Jordan signed the tab.

No words were exchanged between the two for a long time. Gina sipped the iced fruit juice, wishing she *had* escaped to her room. Jordan Gentry was appraising her in a manner that made her skin crawl. He had been obviously startled by the fact that she didn't drink. Gina hadn't offered her personal reasons, but she noticed Jordan's blue gaze sweeping over her to settle on the small gold cross at the base of her throat, and the matching earrings in her pierced lobes. She watched as the knowledge dawned in his eyes.

Whatever Jordan Gentry might have thought of her at the beginning, the impression seemed to have been distorted by his new perception of her. Now that Jordan knew she was a Christian, a woman of faith and principles, he seemed to have nothing more to say!

Gina thought he looked decidedly uncomfortable and she found herself feeling sorry for him. Jordan surveyed the plush room as if he hoped to find a polite topic of conversation lurking nearby. Finding none, Jordan slipped a gold cigarette case from an inner pocket and idly threw it down on the table between them, an open invitation for Gina to accept one if she desired.

"Sorry! I don't smoke, either."

Jordan ducked his chin to light his own cigarette with an ornately engraved lighter. He exhaled a stream of hazy smoke and toyed with the lighter. For a moment his eyes seemed faraway and thoughtful, then he returned to the present with a rueful grin.

"Be glad you don't smoke," he murmured. "It's a habit I wish I'd never started."

Gradually their conversation resumed. Relieved, Gina felt herself relaxing and sensed that Jordan was again enjoying her company. She hoped that he realized she didn't condemn him for his personal decisions, just as she would like to think that he wouldn't be offended by hers.

Time slipped away as they chatted. Gina found there were many things to admire about Jordan Gentry. One thing that did bother her, however, was the fact that he seemed so . . . domineering!

Beginning with the moment they had met, when Jordan

actually ordered her to accept the streamer, up to the present, Gina had found Jordan Gentry to be a man accustomed to issuing commands and expecting unquestioning compliance. Perhaps men developed such leadership techniques when they headed their own corporations, Gina mused, but quickly decided that wasn't a valid reason. Neither her father nor Luke ever took unfair advantage of their power positions aboard the *Sea Nymph*. Jordan Gentry seemed a man who never asked if he could order.

Even as Gina recognized these traits, she observed other qualities which deepened her feelings of attraction for Jordan. Understanding that a man like Jordan would only scoff at her small-town world and religious beliefs, Gina couldn't understand the tumultuous emotions he had stirred in her.

It was a feeling that went far beyond the surface when she'd first been captivated by Jordan's handsome face and mesmerized by his riveting eyes. Helplessly Gina's pulse raced every time Jordan smiled at her. In spite of herself, she found herself idly wondering what it would be like to have Jordan's lips brush hers. How it would feel to have his strong arms around her. To hear his voice whisper tender words of love.

"Is something wrong?"

Jordan's question snapped Gina from her fantasies. A blush crept upwards to stain her cheeks. When she realized that he detected it, she flushed even deeper.

"No, nothing's wrong," Gina said. She avoided his eyes. "I was just thinking that I really should be getting to my stateroom."

Jordan nodded as he picked up the drink he'd scarcely touched. Gina followed his glance to the outer deck where his attention was captured by a stunning blonde, who lingered near the entrance as if she were waiting for someone.

The woman was small but her figure was voluptuous, and she dressed to accentuate the fact. Her skin was a rich honey. Her moonlight blond hair was as thick and lush as a lion's mane. The beautiful woman had the looks and figure many women only hoped to possess. When the woman glanced around, startled by the intensity of Jordan's eyes on her, her china-doll blue eyes widened in delight.

The words on Jordan's lips faded away as a sensuous, inviting smile spread across the beauty's carmine lips. Knowing the enticing picture she presented, she looked away, tossed her silken hair over her slim shoulders, and tipped her face into the caressing wind.

With effort, Jordan found and finished his remark to Gina and she replied, but her words trailed away when she realized Jordan was scarcely listening.

His eyes had returned to the stunning blonde. Compared to the polished, pampered beauty, Gina felt stodgy and plain in the neat dress she and Maureen had decided would be suitable for making the transition from city streets to a cruise ship atmosphere.

"I really must be going." Gina clutched her purse and left the table. "Finish your drink. I can find my way to my quarters."

Jordan started to protest, but Gina brushed by him before he could mouth meaningless, polite phrases. Gina felt Jordan Gentry's eyes on her as she left, but she didn't look back. It wasn't necessary. In her heart Gina knew that the gorgeous blonde would be graciously accepting the seat she'd just vacated. And the realization hurt! More than Gina dreamed it would.

Gina reached for her room key and paused outside the door. Her mind churned. She had no doubt that Jordan's suggestion that they were old friends was a worn-out line he had found useful with women. Jordan should have looked closer before making his pitch, Gina thought wryly. It wouldn't have taken long to figure out they were as different as day and night. Gina obviously wasn't his type and Jordan wasn't the kind of man she should be interested in. She knew that—just as surely as she knew that her heart ached already at the thought of Jordan Gentry smiling across the table at the lovely blonde.

"There you are!" Maureen's voice held a timbre of delight. "Hugh and I have been looking all over the ship for you!"

Maureen, with a slim, well-dressed man in tow, rushed up to Gina. The man's dark brown hair was slightly streaked with gray at the temples, although his skin was tan, smooth, and youthful. Smile lines that suggested a sense of humor crinkled the corners of his brown eyes.

"Hugh, this is the wonderful girl I've been telling you about!" Maureen rushed on in a torrent of words. "The girl I've been promising you'd meet!"

"Maureen!" Gina protested.

The tall brunette smiled blandly in the face of the warning look Gina shot her.

"Gina, this is Hugh Powers," Maureen continued smoothly. "Hugh is an old friend of my family's, although I must admit we haven't seen each other in years." Hugh and Gina shook hands. "Gina's the girl who's treating me to the cruise. Isn't she the perfect friend?"

"Very nice for both of you," Hugh said.

Hugh looked at Gina with renewed interest and admiration and smiled at her in a conspiratorial way, while Maureen rattled on, singing their praises. Gina returned the smile, relieved to know Hugh was amused, rather than disturbed, by Maureen's obvious attempt at matchmaking.

When Hugh later suggested he accompany them to dinner that night, Maureen instantly accepted for both of them.

"I'll be back after I get settled into my stateroom," he promised.

"Terrific!" Maureen said. "Hugh, I can't begin to tell you how glad I am you're on this cruise! Mother and Dad will love to have news of you again."

"Give them my best," Hugh said.

Maureen gave Hugh a fond smile. "I will. I can also tell them you haven't aged a day since we saw you last."

Hugh looked pleased. "You, dear girl, *have* changed. But most becomingly." Hugh turned to Gina. "The last time I saw Maureen she was a coltish girl of seventeen or so. All arms and legs."

"And braces," Maureen reminded, grimacing.

Hugh nodded and laughed at the memory. "Braces like the grillwork of a car," he teased.

Maureen closed the stateroom door behind Hugh and turned to regard Gina with a smug grin.

"Gina, Hugh thinks you're wonderful!" Maureen ran her fingers through her wavy hair and collapsed into a comfortable chair. A musing smile curved Maureen's mouth. "It's really a small world. Imagine my meeting Hugh after all these years!"

"You know him well?" Gina asked.

"Ummmm . . . well enough," Maureen said. "As well as you ever really get to know the other passengers on these cruises. He was a regular for quite a number of winters when my family vacationed. Hugh was as much a part of the cruise as the lifeboats on board. He was like . . . a fixture."

"What does Hugh do for a living?"

Maureen, who'd begun to unpack, halted—a perplexed look on her face. "Now that you ask—I really don't know." Maureen brushed her hair away from her oval face and bent over her suitcase. "Judging from the way Hugh dresses and the fact that he's still roaming the globe—

whatever it is, he does it successfully. Hugh comes from an old-line family with pots of money. I wouldn't be surprised if Hugh doesn't live off the interest from money earned by the sweat of some ancestral brow.''

"He seems pleasant."

"He is. He seems to like you, Gina.'' Maureen straightened up and faced her friend. "You could certainly do worse than Hugh Powers. He's considered a real catch. On past cruises Hugh never lacked for female companionship. Many a wealthy mother with a homely daughter looked with envy on Hugh's companions. I suspect Hugh's at an age where he's been giving some thought to marrying and settling down.'' Maureen giggled. "Knowing you had Hugh in your sights would be a great comfort to your Aunt Nell!''

Gina laughed, too, but it was strained and her voice quickly grew serious. "Maureen, please don't try to line up a romance for me, okay? I'm not sure I'm ready for any kind of involvement just yet. I'm not looking for love.''

"Well, don't be surprised if you find it.''

"I won't find love—love will have to find me!''

Gina thought about love and what it was. She knew she didn't have any accurate standards by which to measure such an elusive emotion. Gina wondered how it felt to truly love and be loved in return. Undoubtedly, when it happened, it would be wonderful—just the way God planned it to be.

Until the time love touched her heart, Gina knew she would have to wonder and wait, knowing that, somewhere, a man waited for her. A man she would recognize as her true love. A man Gina would know returned fully her deepest feelings.

As far as Gina knew, such a possibility was well into the future. At the moment she didn't need well-meaning souls bothering her with introductions to "eligible" men. Men who might look to the rest of the world like Mr. Right, but, for a woman like Gina, couldn't be more wrong. Men who might have everything but the very things Gina needed in a man—faith in God and a tender, loving heart.

CHAPTER 7

FOLLOWING MAUREEN'S REMARKS about Hugh, Gina noticed
that his eyes rested on her with tender respect when he
accompanied the two women to dinner. With mixed emotions, Gina admitted to herself that Maureen was right about
Hugh's feelings for her. Gina was pleased that Hugh
seemed attracted to her. She felt comfortable with him.
What bothered her was that she did not feel for Hugh the
magnetic, consuming attraction she'd instantly felt for Jordan Gentry.

The cuisine was exceptional. Diners said the menu
rivaled the creations of chefs from famous, world-reknowned
restaurants, and the offerings were extraordinary even by
cruise ship standards.

After dessert and a second cup of coffee, Hugh, his eyes
on Gina, suggested they sample the night life in one of the
lounges. He gave Maureen a smile that automatically included her in their plans. When Gina remained silent,
Maureen gave her a speculative look. Correctly interpreting
Gina's hesitation, she was quick to accept the invitation for
both of them.

"Of course!" Maureen agreed, and picked up her purse. "The night is still young!"

"On a cruise ship, everything really comes to life at night," Hugh explained to Gina.

The three found a table in the lounge that was fast filling with passengers seeking the more intimate atmosphere. Several couples were dancing to the enticing rhythms of the excellent band.

"Let's go to the ladies' room," Maureen whispered to Gina shortly after they were seated.

"But I don't . . ."

Gina broke off her words when a delicate frown disturbed Maureen's brow and Gina realized that the girl wanted a chance to speak to her alone.

"What did you want to talk to me about?" Gina asked, when they had retired to the privacy of the powder room.

Maureen took a lipstick from her purse. "I wanted to ask about that handsome man in the dining room—the tall, dark-haired guy. The one who kept watching you like a hawk. He didn't miss a move you made!"

Gina felt a prickly sensation crawl over her skin and advance to her scalp. "A man? Watching *me?*"

Maureen met Gina's eyes in the mirror, nodding, as she traced on her lipstick and pressed her lips together. She studied the effect.

"Uh-huh! He was a real looker, too . . ."

Gina's thoughts automatically flew to Jordan Gentry, the. instantly discarded the idea. When she had left Jordan, he'd hardly have been looking at her in the manner Maureen suggested. Besides, Gina hadn't noticed Jordan in the dining room when she glanced around.

"Tall, dark, handsome," Gina laughed with what she hoped was a casual air. "That probably describes half the men on board."

Maureen nodded reluctantly. "So it does," she admitted. "I was hoping you could tell me who he was, though. I'll tell you what—if we see him again, I'll be sure to point him out to you."

When they returned to the table, the dance floor was crowded with gently swaying couples. Hugh signaled the waiter to come for their order.

"What'll it be?" Hugh asked.

Maureen named her favorite drink. Hugh's eyes swung questioningly to Gina.

"Fruit punch," Gina said. She raised her eyes to Hugh's. "I don't drink."

Hugh's expression was understanding, not judgmental. "I'm not much of a drinker myself," he confided, and turned to the waiter to give the order: Maureen's mixed drink—and two fruit punches.

During the evening meal Hugh and Maureen had reminisced about past cruises and mutual friends. By the time the threesome adjourned to the lounge, the two had covered a great deal of past history, and Gina was now included in the easy conversation.

Well-traveled, Hugh was an amusing storyteller and seemed to have an outlandish tale for almost every port in the world. With Gina and Maureen for an eager audience, he warmed to the situation and entertained them with humorous anecdotes. Gradually, as the atmosphere in the lounge livened, the intensified music punctuated by the clink of glasses made conversation almost impossible.

Not yet finished with their drinks, and unwilling to leave, the three silently watched the dancers. Gina's private thoughts were far from the present moment when Maureen nudged and subtly nodded in the direction of the entrance to the lounge.

"Gina! That's the man!" Maureen silently mouthed the message.

Curious, Gina's eyes swung to follow Maureen's gaze. Her throat tightened when she recognized Jordan Gentry. Abruptly she wrenched her eyes away from him and stared straight ahead. Though Gina didn't dare look toward Jordan again, Maureen did.

"Gina!" Maureen hissed under her breath. "He saw you. He's on his way over!"

Gina fought the compelling urge to look up and pretended a calm she did not feel as she sipped her juice. But her heart was hammering so furiously that she felt as if she were going to faint.

Hugh who had observed Jordan's approach, rose to motion him to their table. "Jordan Gentry—you rascal!" Hugh said, laughing heartily. "I haven't seen you in years, Jordy. You look terrific. Join us!"

With a polite glance at Maureen, and an almost imperceptible nod in Gina's direction, he accepted Hugh's invitation.

"You're looking well yourself, Hugh. It's been a long time since I saw you last. How long has it been?"

"Ten years?" Hugh answered the question with a query of his own, then shrugged. "I've kept track of you through the financial page in the newspapers," Hugh said.

Jordan smiled at the thought. "I'm surprised you have time, Hugh," Jordan chided. "I should think your own dealings would keep you well occupied."

Hugh, flushing, waved the remark aside, and seemed relieved to change the subject.

"Jordan, I don't believe you've met the two lovely ladies at my table."

Maureen flashed Jordan a gracious smile. Gina, not daring to look at the handsome man beside her, pretended occupation with a small circle of moisture that had formed beneath the frosty glass of fruit punch. Jordan perceived her distress, and amusement glittered in his knowing eyes.

"As a matter of fact, Miss Roberts and I have met." Gina glanced up in time to see his eyes flick over her for an instant before they shifted to Maureen. "However, I haven't had the pleasure of meeting Miss . . ." He waited for the introduction.

"Lamkin," Hugh supplied. "Maureen Lamkin. The Lamkins are well known in the fashion and clothing business. Maureen's an old friend of mine." Hugh turned to the brunette. "Maureen, Jordan's with Gentry Enterprises. His company owns a large line of products and equipment for shipping—freight or pleasure cruises. He is constantly expanding in new areas of related interest."

When Gina's gaze met Maureen's, the signal in the tall green-eyed girl's eyes was unmistakable. Maureen was shocked that Gina hadn't mentioned her meeting with Jordan Gentry. Mixed with that look was one of admiration that her small-town friend had already struck up an acquaintance with a man who was wealthy enough to buy and sell anyone on board the ship—perhaps a dozen times over!

With Jordan at their table, the plans Gina and Maureen had made for leaving the crowded, smoky lounge were abandoned. Gradually other guests left the room and the couples waltzing on the dance floor thinned. Maureen lightly tapped her foot in time with the music. Hugh, finally noticing, asked Maureen to dance. With a quick glance over her shoulder at Gina, Maureen followed Hugh to the dance floor.

Alone with Jordan, Gina, who had managed to hold her own with the others nearby, was suddenly overwhelmed by a nervousness that tied her tongue. From the way Jordan stared into his whiskey glass and avoided looking at her, she sensed he was suffering the same discomfort.

At length Jordan turned to Gina. Hastily she looked away, but Jordan's almost mocking gaze drew Gina back and held her eyes captive to his as a slow smile curved his sensual lips.

"You don't smoke, Gina. You don't drink." His voice was subdued. "I'm almost afraid to ask . . . but do you, by any chance, dance?"

Gina almost laughed in her relief at the serious question. "Yes, Jordan, I dance. But, I'm afraid, not very well."

Jordan slid his chair back, took Gina's hand, and drew her toward the dance floor before she could protest, change her mind, or offer an excuse to avoid the circle of his arms.

"Let me be the judge of that," Jordan suggested as he swirled Gina into his arms and captured her in a pleasantly snug embrace.

Gina suffered a moment's hesitation, an instant of awkward uncertainty, before her movements smoothly followed Jordan's. A few minutes later Gina was surprised to find that her pulse had returned to its normal rate.

Jordan was pleased when Gina didn't suggest they return to the table when the number ended. He held her as they danced to another song. And another. Jordan could feel through his fingertips that Gina's form, which had been so rigid at his first touch, had grown relaxed and pliant as they swayed to the beat of the band.

Under the pretense of drawing Gina close to let a nearby couple pass, Jordan momentarily pressed her soft, feminine form against him and thrilled at the contact of her innocent body, producing a moment of pleasure unlike any he'd ever known.

Jordan was accustomed to keeping up a steady line of conversation on the dance floors of the world. With Gina, he felt oddly wordless, though he sensed that his silence did not dismay her. He marveled at the thought that two people, almost strangers, could communicate without the need for words.

Jordan studied the girl in his arms—russet hair feathering away from a smooth brow and hugging the curves of her cheeks. When Gina lowered her topaz eyes, he admired the natural beauty of the fringe of long, dark lashes. Then Jordan's eyes fell to the small gold cross that nestled a few inches above where he suspected the soft cleft of Gina's breasts began. At the thought, Jordan forced his attention elsewhere.

"You lied to me, Gina," Jordan's voice was mockingly stern.

Gina's eyes flipped up to meet his, growing larger with surprise, until she discovered he was teasing. Her questioning look prompted him to explain.

"You told me you weren't a good dancer. On the contrary, you're excellent."

Gina received the compliment with a smile. "Thanks, but if I am, it's only because I don't often have such a good partner."

Amused, Jordan halted, held Gina at arm's length for a fleeting second before he gave her a crooked smile and his eyes played over her wholesome features.

"In that case, my dear girl, then we'd better dance now while you have the chance!"

Gina laughed in response to his light teasing and did not resist when Jordan pulled her close once more. She didn't resist. Couldn't resist! For once in her life Gina was being held in a man's strong embrace where she felt she truly belonged.

"I have my own selfish motives, Gina. I don't just want to give you a chance to dance with an . . . excellent partner. Now that I have you to myself," Jordan's voice was soft and husky, "I won't let you get away—escape—so easily again. Not like you did this afternoon. I don't want to have to share you with Maureen and Hugh. Or . . . anyone.''

Gina was shaken by the low, hoarse intensity of Jordan's words and the almost savage desire glinting in his indigo eyes.

She stiffened in his arms. "Who said I was trying to 'escape' this afternoon?" Unwillingly her thoughts returned to her hasty departure and the blonde waiting her chance to take Gina's place.

Jordan's eyes were a mockery in blue. "Weren't you?"

"I came here with Hugh and Maureen," Gina said, lamely changing the topic. "We should return to the table so I can be with them."

Jordan was silent. "Just because you came here with them—does that mean you feel obligated to leave with them as well? I've always heard it said that two's company and three's a crowd. Two and two, Gina, make four. That's what we are. Unless you owe Hugh something. Do you?"

Gina honestly assessed her feelings for Maureen's friend who had rapidly become her friend as well.

"No, not really. He's a friend of Maureen's family."

"Then you've no reason not to leave with me," Jordan said decisively. "Let's go."

Gina's blood froze. She feared the assumptions Jordan Gentry might be making. He felt her body grow rigid.

"There's no reason for you not to leave with me—unless you'd rather not," Jordan explained. "All I want is your company, Gina. I won't ask for more than you can freely give. Whatever you want is what I want. What'll it be?" Jordan forced her decision. "Stay here with Hugh and Maureen . . . or leave with me?"

Jordan saw the answer in Gina's golden eyes before it formed on her lips. Without a word he cupped her elbow and guided her back to the table. Gina avoided Hugh as she hastily explained she was leaving with Jordan. Jordan wondered at the feelings that had already developed between the two. In Hugh's eyes he found one answer; in Gina's actions, another.

As the couple left the noisy lounge, an uneasy silence fell between them. Out on the upper deck, Jordan didn't reach for Gina's hand or slip his arm around her waist as he had intended. He sensed that Gina was as surprised to find herself with him as he was to have her so easily at his side.

Casting Gina a sideways glance, Jordan took pleasure once more in her unspoiled beauty. Gina's personality had affected him that afternoon, but the aura of innocent loveliness and her ability to carry on an intelligent conversation without resorting to coy innuendos fascinated him.

The first moment Jordan had seen her, he had been intent on arranging an introduction that could lead to a shipboard fling. Then he realized there was something hauntingly familiar about Gina. Jordan wracked his brain, trying to recall if Gina were one of the many women whose company he had enjoyed in the past, then had just as quickly forgotten when they parted.

When Gina assured him they had not met, his first instinct was disbelief. But a short while later, he decided she must be telling the truth and that she was the victim of mistaken identity. Or, perhaps he'd seen the girl on the streets of New York City and remembered her. Though he might forget *where* he had known a woman, he rarely forgot a beautiful face.

Jordan's initial plans for seduction had almost been abandoned when he discovered Gina's spirituality. Jordan was amazed that he hadn't observed it right from the start. But Gina's looks and actions were deceiving. She was certainly not like the church women from his childhood—who could mouth pious phrases one moment and juicy gossip the next.

From all outward appearances Gina was as appealing and attractive as any woman. It wasn't until they were in the lounge and he had presumed too much about her that Gina had revealed the level of her Christian commitment.

Jordan grimaced at the embarrassing memory, then broke the silence: "Have you seen the ship?"

Gina shook her head. "Not all of it."

Jordan halted and touched the solid railing with a gesture not unlike an affectionate pat.

"I once worked on this old girl. I was part of the crew. It seems a century ago. Ten years back I knew this ship from the Captain's quarters to the boiler room." Jordan looked down at her and Gina saw a flood of memories rush back to engulf him. A look of nostalgia gave way to a rueful grin. "Believe me, Gina, I much prefer the status of paying guest to that of a position with the paid crew."

Gina's light laughter mingled with his. "I shouldn't doubt that! The service on board is extraordinary."

"With one crew member for every two guests, it should be."

"I'm afraid some guests take the service for granted," Gina said. "They don't really appreciate the crew's efforts."

"Speaking from my own experience, I'd have to agree with you. But don't misunderstand me," Jordan amended, "I wouldn't trade those times I spent working aboard ships for anything. Much of what I learned then has helped me make my business the success it has become."

At Gina's urging Jordan told her much more about his business than she'd been able to pick up from Hugh's casual comments. He explained how the enterprise had grown from a small investment to a large, solid company constantly bringing out innovative new equipment.

When Jordan finished explaining his rise in the shipping

world, Gina spoke. "You've done well. Hugh admires you very much."

A brooding expression clouded Jordan's sharply chiseled features. "I suppose some people would say I've done well with my life," Jordan murmured, but the tone in his voice seemed sadly despairing. Gina sensed that Jordan Gentry's success was somehow blighted by unrelenting feelings of failure. She remained silent in order to allow Jordan to speak further, and felt an odd sense of disappointment when he chose not to continue.

Instead, he took Gina's hand and led her along the lonely teakwood deck. Much time and a great deal of talk later, it was at Gina's reluctant suggestion that they began moving in the direction of her stateroom.

When they neared a dark alcove on deck, and Jordan purposely halted, Gina's heart thudded crazily. Gina knew Jordan wanted to kiss her every bit as much as she wanted him to.

For a split second Jordan stared into Gina's eyes—large and luminous in the reflected light, so close to his, so trusting, so full of questions, yet holding a gentle invitation.

In her eyes Jordan recognized the moment when Gina gave in to her desires. Gina's long lashes fluttered shut as her eyes closed and she tipped her tender lips in offering to his. Jordan's pulse skipped to an erratic beat when Gina Roberts moved, warm and yielding, into his arms. The message of Gina's mouth answered the demands on his lips. Reckless, rash emotions swept over him, pulling him down into a whirling eddy of desire. Jordan was lost in the pleasure of the kiss, wanting the contact to go on and on, never ending, when Gina moved restlessly in his arms. Jordan refused to let her go.

"Gina . . . Gina . . ." Jordan murmured her name, drugged by the sweetness of her kisses.

"Jordan!"

Gina's protest was a soft whisper that dissolved into a weak moan as she breathed his name over and over, her fingertips touching the back of his neck as his lips nuzzled the hollow of her throat, then found her mouth again. She wanted him as surely as he wanted her! Yet, there came a moment when her resolve firmed. Desperately she tried to wrench herself away. He felt the fright catapulting through her lithe form as she tried to pry her lips from his. He would not allow it! His strong hand crept to the nape of her neck and, vise like, held Gina a prisoner to his emotions.

Gina struggled against him but Jordan was stronger. So much stronger. An instant later, he relished the moment when Gina's weakness signaled his conquest.

Then, in a sudden revelation, Jordan realized exactly what he was doing . . . and to whom! A woman like Gina! He couldn't go through with it—much as he wanted to.

Somehow, abruptly, with the impact of a crystal goblet shattering on a terra cotta floor, Jordan released Gina. He stared at her harshly in the moonlight as he gasped to catch his breath. The way Gina looked up at him, so innocent, so unaware, he wanted to shake her! But Jordan knew if he touched her again there would be no turning back. She was so vulnerable standing there, looking into his eyes, her lips parted . . .

"What's the idea . . . kissing me like that? Can't you see . . ." Jordan's self-directed anger was vented on Gina before his words trailed off. But she did not understand.

Stricken, Gina blinked. Quick tears of rejection and humiliation sprang to her eyes.

"I-I don't know what came over me," Gina hurriedly choked out an apology. "It must've been the moonlight. I'm sorry. I hate to think what you must think of me now . . ."

Before Jordan could realize Gina's intentions, make a move to protest, or clear up her mistaken assumption, she turned and darted away. Shocked and shaken, he could only stare after her.

There was no sense chasing after her to explain, he decided. What was the use? How could he express his conflicting feelings to her when he couldn't begin to understand them himself?

For a long while Jordan stood at the railing and stared into the inky water below as he tried to sort out his feelings. Jordan was sorely tempted to go to Gina's stateroom and bang on the door until she let him in. Perhaps in the rush of words, his own self-knowledge would come.

Jordan abandoned the idea. With any other woman he would have pursued that course of action and they would have laughed together over the foolish moment. But Gina was different. Jordan's heart ached with heaviness when he realized that with a mouthful of careless, poorly chosen, inaccurate words, he had made Gina Roberts feel ugly, rejected, and disgusting—when all she'd dared to do was reveal the tender, vulnerable emotions of love locked in her gentle heart.

Jordan knew that he had hurt Gina, but the pain was mostly his. Hurting her was the last thing Jordan wanted to do, yet somehow it seemed to be the first thing he accomplished whenever he was with her.

CHAPTER 8

GINA CLOSED HER stateroom door behind her and leaned against it, fighting to catch her breath. The door was cool against her warm skin, and it solidly supported her as her breath came in painful jerks. She wiped her eyes before pinching them shut against the burning dampness of tears and lifted her face to remember the last few minutes with Jordan that would forever mar the beautiful memories of their evening together.

It seemed incredible to her that she'd actually thrown herself into Jordan Gentry's arms like some love-struck schoolgirl. Where Jordan was involved, Gina felt like a puppet on a string. It was as if irresistible outside forces had propelled her into his arms. Gina hadn't known if she had moved toward Jordan or if he had come to her, but once she found herself in his arms, it had felt so right.

Then came the awful moment when Jordan broke away and stared at her. His shocking speech still rang in her ears—words that had been indelibly burned into her memory. Like a broken record, each time she replayed them she suffered fresh shame.

Shaking her head in despair, Gina flipped on the lamp and crossed the room. Maureen was already sleeping, and Gina was thankful her friend did not awaken to question her.

In order to escape her punishing thoughts, Gina concentrated on the mundane procedure of readying for bed. Slipping between the sheets, she reached for her Bible. Gina opened to the marker, but the words swirled before her eyes. The only idea that registered was the belief that Jordan Gentry thought she was some kind of . . . conniving tramp!

With Jordan's incredible good looks and wealth, he probably had women falling at his feet wherever he went. In exchange for the things he could offer—money, prestige, and the advantage of being seen with such a powerful man—many women had probably offered themselves to him. A man like Jordan would have to be on guard to avoid compromising situations staged by wily women on the make!

But that wasn't Gina's intention. With her hands resting on the open Bible in her lap, she analyzed her feelings for the handsome businessman. In her heart she knew that loving him was wrong. Wrong! How could it be right when everything about Jordan Gentry ran counter to what she believed, wanted, and needed.

Yet never before had she responded to any man like she had to Jordan. No wonder he suspected her of ulterior motives. There had been promises in her kisses that Gina knew she could never keep. Tears burned in her eyes. Why did it have to be like this? Why did she have to feel so very much in love when she knew that a romance with Jordan Gentry was not meant to be?

The Bible slipped shut between Gina's trembling hands. Maybe she was being tested. Maybe she was being tried to see if her faith was strong enough to resist a man like Jordan Gentry so she could appreciate more fully the man she was meant to love.

Bitter tears scalded Gina's eyes as she forced her lips, and then her heart, to offer a pleading prayer to God that she would be able to follow His way and not seek her own. Gina prayed that the mistaken feelings she had for Jordan would be erased from her heart so she would remain open to accept and recognize the love of the man God had chosen for her.

When Gina opened her eyes, they were moist with unshed tears. Maureen rolled over in bed, sat up, squinted at her watch, then stared across at Gina.

"You finally got in," Maureen said, her voice husky with sleep. "I was about to get worried. I'd intended to wait up for you, but I was so tired I dozed off."

"Wait up? Whatever for? Don't you trust me?" Gina quipped in a light voice. Maureen wasn't taken in.

"You, Gina, I trust. But after what Hugh told me about Jordan. . . . well, the infamous Jordan Gentry I do *not* trust!"

At the words Gina's chest constricted so tightly that it was hard to breathe. She licked her lip nervously. "What did Hugh say?"

Maureen answered with an expressive roll of her eyes and twitch of her mouth. "It might be easier to tell you what he *didn't* say!"

Gina paused. "Hugh must've given you an earful of information."

"Did he!" Maureen cried. "Hugh was positively beside himself when you left with Jordan. Jordan, Hugh says, has an awful reputation with women—a real playboy. He switches women the way other men change socks!" Maureen hesitated. "Hugh really cares for you, Gina. He thinks the sun rises and sets in you. He was worried sick when you left with Jordan, but I finally convinced him that you have too much good sense and decency to be taken in by the smooth line of some fast-talking skirt-chaser." Maureen paused. "Did he . . . try anything?"

"No," Gina said and avoided Maureen's eyes. "Really, nothing happened. I'm sorry you and Hugh were so worried. I'm tired. Let's get some sleep, okay?"

"Sure," Maureen said. She sensed that Gina had no wish to discuss the evening further. "Whatever you want. G'night, Gina."

Gina switched off the lamp and plunged the stateroom into darkness. She tried to continue with her prayers, but the memory of the scene with Jordan, and now Maureen's words conveying Hugh's opinion of Jordan overshadowed all other thoughts.

Gina suspected Hugh was right about Jordan. She was out of her league with a man like him. He had undoubtedly kissed hundreds of women with no more meaning or commitment than he'd felt when he kissed her. The thought offered no consolation. Instead it only increased the dull, throbbing ache in Gina's heart.

While Gina drifted off to sleep, Jordan stood alone on the upper deck, smoking and thinking. A strange combination of reluctance and relief settled over him now that he was alone again.

Part of him wanted to go after Gina—even as another side of his nature knew that he had to get away from her influence in order to think, to question, to rage bitterly against the odd purpose of her entanglement in his life. Jordan didn't need Gina's feelings, her emotions, her beliefs clouding his judgment while he sought his own answers to the question that had never been far from his mind since receiving an invitation to visit an old friend for the holidays. Then, like a coward, he had backed out at the last minute.

When Jordan accepted the invitation, he had looked forward to the reunion—that is, before the moment of introspection. For the first time Jordan saw clearly the man he had gradually become in the intervening years—a man far different from the school chum his friend would be expecting. He feared he could not face his trusted mentor as he was. Not now.

His friend, Jordan knew, would never reproach him—would never judge him. No. In an honest moment, Jordan Gentry had to admit that he, himself, was his own problem.

Since Christmas, Jordan felt as if he had been stalled at the crossroads in his life, unable to decide which way to turn. He sensed he couldn't continue on the path he'd been following, but he was reluctant to make another choice.

A never-ending feeling of pressure and strain convinced Jordan he needed a vacation—time away from ringing telephones, business conferences, social obligations, and the relentless hounding of his conscience. Ironically everywhere he turned, he found Gina Roberts and her faith to serve as a constant reminder of the decision he'd tried to avoid.

In his better moments when he was with Gina, Jordan savored the serenity and peace that he knew could be his if he turned back to Christ and accepted the forgiveness available to repentant prodigal sons. Jordan had experienced that sensation before the cruise, too. But it seemed that, every time he was strongly tempted to return to the ways of the Word, worldly cares distracted him and the important decision he faced was pigeon-holed indefinitely. For Jordan, this verdict was not one that could be reached by someone else. In his business, when faced by a knotty problem, he often hired an expert to research the area and suggest the solution. This decision, however, was one only he could give, freely, and of his own will.

Jordan's thoughts flipped back through recent years. Sometimes it seemed a lifetime since he'd started his walk with God instead of only a few years.

Many people, and these now included Gina, had alluded to his successful life. But Jordan knew the truth. He'd made a mess of things! God had blessed him, and to show his appreciation, he had hardened his heart, accepting and turning toward the world and all it offered even as he deliberately turned away from the Light of the World.

In Gina's company Jordan was reminded of the faith that had once been his. He was confronted by the true image of the worldly man he had become. Yet, in spite of all of this, Jordan knew that Gina Roberts truly cared for him. What she didn't seem to know—or could not see—was that Jordan had the capacity to destroy her, sully her innocence, ruin her faith. Jordan knew his effect on her, just as Gina seemed blissfully unaware of her gentle influence over him.

For a moment Jordan's thoughts soared with hope, and he wondered if he could yet become the kind of man deserving of a good woman like Gina. A man who could once again be unswerving in his faith. A man who could live by the principles he'd since abandoned. A man who drew his strength from Scripture and trustingly followed where his Lord led him.

Jordan's sudden hopes faded when he reviewed the many pleasures he would have to renounce forever in order to claim Gina for his own. He was not sure he could do it . . . or that Gina was worth it. What if he found out that he tired of her as he had eventually tired of all the women who had come and gone in his life? What if he found that, after returning control of his life to Christ, he was no better, no stronger, than he'd proven to be the first time? Would he backslide and fall away again?

Years before, when Jordan had witnessed to his friends of

his spiritual awakening, they had been skeptical. A few scoffed openly. Some expressed the opinion that it was a phase he was going through, assuring him that he'd get over it and when he came to his senses, he would again be the same old Jordan. Hotly he had denied it. Jordan tried to explain the special feeling of his new-found relationship with the Lord. But most of them remained unconvinced. And now, it appeared that their words had been prophetic. He *had* fallen away, along with others who had made the same profession. Sometimes, idly, Jordan wondered if all the others who'd wandered away from the Lord ever felt the gentle call to return that he often did, however fleetingly.

What about Gina? Would he be able to remain faithful with a woman like Gina serving as a supportive influence? Or was Gina, too, experiencing a religious stage in her life? Would she, too, turn her back one day and fall away?

Was the intensity of her kiss an unintentional signal that she was chafing at her religious bonds, straining to be freed by the love of a flesh-and-blood man? The image of Gina giving herself to him sent his blood coursing hotly in his veins, until the tender vision was erased from his mind, to be replaced by the tawdry recollection of a pudgy, towel-wrapped stockbroker at the Club. Once, when religion had become a topic of steam room conversation, this man, with a knowing wink, had informed the younger members that it was the prim and pious girls who could be the most passionate when you finally got them to let their hair down.

Jordan suspected the aging man might be right. Without knowing why, Jordan fervently hoped he was not. He hoped Gina wasn't like some Christians, who mouthed one set of principles in public, but privately lived by another.

Candidly, as was his custom, Jordan weighed his choices. He wanted Gina! She would be good for him. So very good. But he knew he could be a destructive influence in her life. For the first time in he didn't know how long, Jordan closed his eyes against the ocean of darkness and prayed to God, asking for guidance.

The prayer was a rambling series of thoughts as he requested the strength to resist giving in to his manly nature and human desires, and for the strength and will power to stay away from Gina Roberts before his temptations could . . .

"Got a moment, Jordan, old friend?"

From the depths of his strange prayer, Jordan was forced back to the present moment by the sound of Hugh Powers' voice.

"Of course," Jordan murmured. "What can I do for you?"

Hugh hesitated. "I've got a rather embarrassing favor to ask."

"Ask away. It's yours," Jordan promised.

"I was unusually busy and I left New York without realizing that I was short of cash. I'll have to wire . . ."

"You need some money? No trouble at all," Jordan assured him as he pulled out his wallet, extracted some bills, then tucked it away. Jordan mused that it was often true that the wealthiest of people often ended up borrowing cash from others because they didn't have the foresight to take care of such mundane matters.

"Maybe some day I can return the favor," Hugh said.

Jordan gave Hugh a studied glance as a quick solution to his dilemma dawned. When Jordan spoke, it was with carefully measured words.

"You can do me one right now."

"Now? What?" Hugh asked.

Jordan's feelings seesawed. He was about to spill the truth: "You can do me a favor by staying out of my way and away from Gina Roberts!" Instead, Jordan swallowed the harsh words and replied mildly. "You can do me a favor by taking Gina Roberts off my hands."

Hugh did a visible doubletake. Hugh had not missed the look in Jordan's eyes when he left the lounge a step behind Gina.

"Jordan, I'm afraid I don't understand." Hugh groped for words.

"She bores me," Jordan lied flatly. "Gina's a nice girl. You know it—I know it. But she's not my kind of woman. If you step in, it might keep things from getting sticky for me."

"You aren't exactly the kind of fellow I was thinking a girl like Gina should be interested in," Hugh admitted.

Jordan bristled at the remark and snorted sarcastically. "And I suppose you are?" He flung the idea in Hugh's face. Before the smaller man could reply, Jordan's voice lost its brittle edge, but only after considerable effort. "Yes, I suppose you are, Hugh," he sighed wearily. "So just keep Gina out of my way."

"What if Gina has other ideas?" Hugh countered.

"She won't," Jordan said confidently. "She's much too refined to chase after a man. Besides, I can tell she likes you, Hugh, just as I know you care for Gina."

Hugh didn't deny it. "I wasn't aware my feelings for Gina were so apparent."

"They are," Jordan replied. "In the long run we'll be helping each other, don't you think?" Hugh's answer was a relieved smile and a quick nod. "Oh, and by the way," Jordan added as an afterthought, "just because I don't want to be romantically involved with the girl doesn't mean I have no interest in her." Jordan turned to face Hugh and his blue eyes flashed like heat lightning across a dark, ominous summer sky. "I don't want Gina Roberts hurt. You, too, have a reputation with the women, Hugh. And if you hurt Gina, I swear you'll answer to me!"

Hugh was unperturbed by the threat. "You worry needlessly, Jordan. I can assure you that my intentions toward Gina are most honorable. Meeting her is like an answer to a prayer. Gina is special. There's a substance and depth to her. She's not like some women. When Gina looks at me, I know she sees me as a person, not a bank account." Hugh turned away and his profile was outlined by the glow of the deck lights. "I'm getting older, Jordan. I've been giving thought to marrying and settling down, but I've never met the right woman. Gina is the type of woman who could keep a man content for life—the kind a man takes home to meet his family."

Jordan's cleft chin stiffened at the seriousness of Hugh's intentions, and he felt unreasonable jealousy erupting within, drowning him in anger.

"Just remember," Jordan warned darkly. "You ever hurt her—ever—and you'll have to reckon with me!"

"I won't hurt her. I could never hurt her . . . any more than you already have."

"What do you mean by that?" Jordan's voice was a whiplash cracking through the stillness of the night.

"Nothing, really. Just an idle comment about the look on Gina's face tonight. She's falling in love with you, Jordan," Hugh murmured. "But maybe that's why you suddenly want no more to do with her. The challenge and thrill of conquest are gone . . ."

Jordan wanted to make a rebuttal, but he feared that his explosive emotions would further complicate things. The anger he felt was more for himself than for Hugh, who had merely dared to speak the truth. Jordan knew what it was they all said about him—that for him the thrill was in the chase—and when the conquest had been made, his interest in a woman ceased.

With a casual wave Hugh moved on. Jordan stared after

him and felt an inappropriate urge to laugh, followed by a deep sense of loss. At that instant Jordan wished that he had not cockily asked Hugh to take Gina off his hands as if she were an excess piece of baggage. With the feat accomplished, he realized he had never wanted her more!

For the first time in years Jordan felt utterly helpless. He turned to retreat to his stateroom, where he could think without further interruption, but decided his own company and thoughts were not the therapy he needed. He moved in the direction of the late-night lounge where the music from the cabaret had created a lively atmosphere.

A drink might help him forget. Or he might meet another woman—a woman who could help him forget his feelings for Gina. A woman who could ease the sweet pain of Gina's love by offering him the momentary fulfillment of another.

Jordan hesitated in the doorway of the cabaret as his eyes adjusted to the bright lights. His gaze swept the room—and he saw her—just as she turned.

China-blue eyes issued a sultry invitation across the crowded room. Danielle Elliot tossed her thick blond hair back over creamy tan shoulders, fetchingly revealed by her daringly low-cut gown. Then Danni parted her lips and gave Jordan a heavy-lidded, beckoning smile. The look of promise in her bold eyes made Jordan forget Gina's tender look of love. Gina Roberts was the woman Jordan wanted—but Danielle was a warm, seductive woman of few scruples, who would be more than happy to help him forget the lady he dared not love.

CHAPTER 9

HUGH POWERS' COFFEE cooled to lukewarm while he stared out over the placid Caribbean, his thoughts dwelling on the strange conversation with Jordan the night before. Things couldn't have worked out better if he had arranged them himself! To have Jordan willingly step out of his way with Gina was like an answered prayer.

Until Jordan strode into the lounge the night before, Hugh had felt confident in winning Gina's love. But his plans and dreams evaporated when he was forced to witness the perfect woman, who'd only hours before walked into his life, leaving with Jordan Gentry. With competition like Jordan, Hugh didn't stand a chance.

Gina hesitated in the doorway of the dining room where early risers were having breakfast. Immediately she noticed Hugh, a heavy scowl contorting his features. Although she was relieved to see a familiar face, Gina was alarmed to discover Hugh in such a grim frame of mind, and she was hesitant about intruding on his thoughts.

Other passengers, noting that Gina was alone, invited her to join them. At their comments Hugh looked up. Seeing

Gina, his frown was replaced by a quick grin, and he insisted she join him.

"Coffee?" Hugh asked. Not waiting for an answer, he summoned the waiter to fill her cup.

"Thanks," Gina smiled at the uniformed crew member and stirred creamy swirls into the dark liquid.

"Is Maureen sleeping in?" Hugh asked.

Gina nodded and took a sip of the steaming brew. "She may as well sleep late while she has the chance. Before we know it, vacation will be over and it'll be back to work for both of us."

"You're not a late sleeper?"

Gina shook her head. "Partly by choice, though. Early morning has always been my favorite hour."

"You, too?" Hugh remarked. "I've always felt that way. It's pleasant to be up and about alone—to think, plan, read, or just dream, while it seems the rest of the world is still sleeping."

"That's a large part of it," Gina agreed. "But getting up early isn't a habit that's easy for a working girl to break. I'm so used to being up at dawn that, even when I do get a chance to sleep late, I wake up like clockwork."

Gina told Hugh about her life back in Maine, Aunt Nell, the *Book Nook,* and even sketched a few colorful stories of Bridgeton's more eccentric characters. Hugh chuckled over the vivid tales and his smiles neatly masked the hint of concern that lay behind his brown eyes. Though Gina noticed his puzzled look, it was gone so quickly she decided she had imagined it.

While Gina spoke, Hugh studied her, hoping his face didn't betray the consternation he was experiencing. Hugh couldn't help feeling hurt that Gina Roberts apparently did not trust him enough to tell him the truth about herself, and he could only wonder why.

In the space of five minutes, Gina had told Hugh a life story that contradicted everything he knew about her. Gina described herself as a bookstore clerk working for a maiden aunt in a small New England town. To hear her tell it, Hugh mused, you'd quickly decide Gina was a poor working girl of modest tastes and limited means. But the picture she presented to the world was quite another matter.

Hugh, who knew fine clothing, recognized the designer creations. Certain tailoring tricks told the origin of the garments as clearly as if Gina had been wearing the expensive labels stitched to her sleeve. A bookstore clerk couldn't begin to afford the clothing Gina wore so casually. Her few pieces of jewelry, while not ostentatious, were of good quality. The matching luggage Hugh had noticed in the girls' stateroom when Maureen introduced him to Gina was top-of-the-line—not the cheap baggage of a young woman on limited income.

Maureen, Hugh knew without doubt, came from a wealthy family. When he'd run across her the day before at a bon voyage party, she'd told him she was on the cruise as the guest of a friend. Bookstore clerks could hardly afford to treat their heiress friends to luxury-liner cruises!

Gina was obviously lying about herself! Buy why? *Why?* He pondered the idea. Why was Gina intent on passing herself off as someone she was not? Why did she want him to view her as a working girl rather than the wealthy young woman from a good family that he surmised her to be?

The disturbing thoughts persisted until Hugh remembered something else Maureen had told him. When Gina and Jordan had left together, Hugh questioned Maureen's look of concern. She explained that Gina had only recently been hurt by a disappointing love affair. Maureen hadn't offered any details, nor had Hugh fished for background. But from the few facts he was able to piece together, Hugh knew that

Gina had been engaged, very briefly, to a young man who turned out to be not at all what she hoped for in a husband.

That had to be the reason, he decided. More than likely the man Gina had loved wanted her for her money and not for herself. That would certainly explain Gina's deceitful posture. If she met a man and fell in love with him, she could then be confident he loved her for the woman she was and not for the easy wealth she represented.

"A penny for your thoughts, Hugh," Gina said softly when several seconds passed and Hugh continued to stare across the vast expanse of water.

Hugh turned to face her with a lazy smile. "You're a terrible cheapskate, my dear. The thoughts I was having about you were worth at least a million dollars . . . or . . . a week's salary at the *Book Nook*."

Gina shrugged it off with a cheerful smile. "I'll have to pass then. Your price is beyond my means."

Hugh laughed. "Then maybe sometime when I'm feeling generous, I'll tell you for free."

A short while later Gina and Hugh left the dining room. They walked in the early morning breeze and basked in the sun, enjoying small talk. Time passed rapidly and the ship came alive, as passengers awakened and set about to relish the activities of the day.

When they neared the pool, where a few sunbathers lolled on chaise lounges, their attention was arrested by a commotion. Gina's heart seemed to cease beating when she recognized a tan body hugged by swimming briefs. It was Jordan, carrying a rumpled blonde to the edge of the pool.

"This will wash the sleep from your eyes, Danni!" Jordan heaved her toward the center of the pool. The girl shrieked, but her cries were drowned out by the splash of water that bubbled over her as she sank beneath the surface. Jordan dove in and helped the woman upright in the water, laughing as she wrung water from her hair.

"Jordan Gentry . . . I—I—I—hate you!" she sputtered.

By her tone it was plain she meant anything but that. Her outburst was greeted by Jordan's mocking laughter.

"You beast!" she fumed. "Apologize to me!" the pretty woman demanded, gazing up through thick, wet lashes to regard Jordan who grinned down at her. The invitation in her eyes was unmistakable, and, as expected, Jordan dropped a light kiss on her pouty lips.

"That's better," the blonde murmured, and her arm slipped possessively around Jordan's slim waist.

Gina turned away. Her feeble attempt to continue their conversation touched Hugh deeply. He saw the hurt in her eyes and recognized the forced brightness in her voice. Hugh was moved by Gina's bravado, but he wanted her to understand that she didn't have to put on a front for his sake. Tenderly he put his arm around Gina's shoulder and gave her an encouraging squeeze. She smiled up at him and blinked fast before she looked away.

"Gina, you'll never know how I wish you hadn't seen that. I'd give anything for you to have been spared."

Gina gave Hugh a weak, unconvincing smile. "It's all right. It doesn't matter. Really, it doesn't."

"Methinks the lady doth prest too much," Hugh murmured. "Of course it matters or you wouldn't look so crushed." Hugh paused in a secluded spot. "Last night, Gina, I know you started to care about Jordan Gentry." Gina looked away, but Hugh's eyes were not to be avoided. "Take my word for it, darling. Jordan's not worth your care and concern. I know he was with you last night. But after he left you, he apparently found another companion. And after this blonde, there will be some other woman. I've known Jordan for many years, and he has earned his reputation. Many say that Jordan is only interested—captivated—by a woman when she seems unattainable. Once she gives in, he quickly loses interest."

Gina flinched. "N-nothing like that happened."

"I know that," Hugh whispered softly. "You're not that kind of woman. You know it. I know it. Even Jordan gave up on you fast, and that proves *he* knows it." Hugh shrugged. "He probably figured he didn't stand a chance with you. Be thankful. Few women can stand in the face of the Gentry charm when Jordan decides to pour it on. Even when women know his ruthless reputation, they walk into bad situations with their eyes open. Each woman probably believes she can break Jordan Gentry's love 'em and leave 'em habit. Each woman no doubt thinks she can hold him where all the others have failed. Until Jordan proves her wrong."

Gina nodded, not knowing what to say, but wishing the topic of conversation would change before she burst into the tears that seemed so near the surface every time she contemplated Jordan Gentry with his golden girl.

"I can't warn a lot of women about a man like Jordan," Hugh went on. "They wouldn't listen. But I feel obligated with a nice girl like you. I don't want Jordan hurting you more than he already has."

"You make him sound heartless."

Hugh thought a moment. "If I do—then that's a mistake. Jordan is a complex man, but he's far from heartless. Jordan is calculating. He's shrewd. He's stubborn. When Jordan decides what he wants, he goes after it and lets nothing and no one stand in his way. Rumor has it that there's yet another side to Jordan—a side that I've never personally seen, I might add. But I'm told he can be a kind, caring, gentle man. If you can believe the idle gossip you hear, some say Jordan Gentry is even a devout and religious man."

"Religious!?"

Hugh smiled at Gina's dramatic reaction. "I see you find that as hard to believe as I." Hugh gave Gina a wry smile. "Perhaps there's nothing to it. It sounds like just the type rumor started by a jilted lover in hopes that other women will avoid Jordan and turn him into a celibate!"

Hugh and Gina spent the rest of the day together. Neither of them mentioned Jordan again, even when they caught sight of him with Danielle Elliot, who was reputed to be the daughter of a wealthy real estate tycoon.

When Hugh walked Gina back to her quarters that night, she wondered nervously what might transpire outside her stateroom door. Gina was relieved when, instead of attempting to kiss her, Hugh merely patted her arm, wished her good-night, and voiced the desire to see her at breakfast the next morning.

Alone in her stateroom Gina reflected on the day with Hugh. She liked him. Hugh was funny, witty, and pleasant to be with. Gina had grown fond of him in a short time. But the truth was she did not feel for Hugh what she suspected he felt for her. A twinge of guilt nagged at her conscience. While Hugh was so attentive, so caring, and so loyal, all her thoughts, her hopes, and her dreams were still held captive by the sweet memory of Jordan Gentry. If only she could feel for Hugh—who'd already asked her to go with him to Sunday services aboard ship—the same wild, reckless, loving emotions she harbored in her heart for Jordan Gentry!

Perhaps Hugh was the man for her. A good man. A decent man. A man who worshipped God openly. Gina's heart wasn't set spinning at the thought of him, but perhaps that was the difference between infatuation and real love. Maybe love—real love—came slowly, softly, almost unnoticed.

The next morning Gina overslept. By the time she arrived

in the dining room, she realized Hugh had probably already been there and gone. The whole ship seemed astir with excitement when the captain piloted the liner through the channels and neared New Providence Island and its capital, Nassau, where they were to be in port for the day.

Even though Gina had missed seeing Hugh for breakfast, she anticipated that they would tour the port together. So when Maureen invited her to go ashore with her and a friend, Roddy Tedrick, Gina declined the offer and explained she had plans with Hugh.

As the ship neared port, Gina hurried to the deck. When guests began streaming from the ship, Gina stood aside and scanned the crowd for Hugh. Soon the passengers departing the *Tropical Star* had thinned to a few stragglers, and Gina wondered if she should have accepted Maureen's and Roddy's offer, after all. She hadn't seen a thing of Hugh! What could be keeping him?

For fifteen more minutes Gina waited while the hands on her watch crawled ahead at an agonizingly slow pace. She was eager to be off and see the sights during the all-too-short port call before the ship set sail again late that night. She frowned. It wasn't like Hugh to be late or to drop from sight without explanation. The niggling thought returned that maybe Hugh hadn't viewed the port-of-call as a date! He had said he'd see her for breakfast, but she'd overslept. Perhaps she had read into his words more than he had intended.

"Waiting for someone?"

The deep, hauntingly familiar voice spoke from directly behind her. Gina whirled, expecting to see Hugh. Instead, it was Jordan Gentry standing so close that when she turned, she lost her balance and stumbled against him. Gina sprang back in surprise. Her eyes shifted from Jordan's mocking gaze to scan the deck in the hope of catching sight of Hugh.

"Expecting someone?" Jordan asked again.

Gina's face grew forlorn even as she tried to force a smile into place.

"No . . . I'm not."

Jordan gave Gina a knowing smile. "Pity!" His tone was cocky. "I was hoping that you were waiting for *me!*"

Gina's cheeks stained a deep rose at the idea that he would suspect her of waiting for him, hoping to finagle him into taking her ashore!

"I—was—only—" Gina choked out a few faltering words before she fell quiet, her silence underscored by the soft slap of waves against the ship.

Jordan had a knack for setting her on edge, especially now that Hugh had given her a profile of his true nature. As Gina considered possible explanations for her presence on deck, she realized almost any answer she could give Jordan would be misinterpreted or distorted.

If she admitted she had been waiting for Hugh, it would appear to Jordan that she had been stood up. And, if she said she had not been waiting for anyone in particular, the egotistical man would probably assume that Gina *had* been stalling in hopes of just such a chance encounter!

Jordan's turquoise eyes continued to assess Gina as he waited for her to formulate her answer. His lips twitched into a half smile, and Gina felt like a frightened mouse, cornered by a much larger, smirking cat.

Gina tilted her head back and thrust her chin forth firmly—almost defiantly. She was determined to remain calm and not let Jordan know the unnerving effect he had on her.

"I—I was enjoying the sunshine. And waiting for the crowds going ashore to thin."

Gina met Jordan's eyes with a look that silently dared him to make some crack. When he spoke his voice was cordial and he suggested they go ashore together. Hesitating, Gina was torn between her desire to be with Jordan and her inner fear of the influence he had over her.

"Come along," Jordan ordered. "We can't stay in the hot sun all morning—no matter how enjoyable you find it. And, as you can see, we seem to have the entire ship to ourselves. Come along, Gina," Jordan spoke with authority. Then his expression softened. "Unless you'd really rather . . . not."

Gina glanced up at him. Her pulse quickened to a crazy calypso beat at the unfamiliar tone in Jordan's voice. Already she'd come to know him as a man who tended to issue orders, with the expectation that they would be carried out, no questions asked.

"I'd like to see Nassau with you," Gina acquiesced. "You probably know the area well and I certainly need a guide."

Jordan made light of his knowledge. "I've been here a number of times," he admitted in an off-hand manner. "I know Nassau well enough to make sure we steer clear of the usual tourist traps."

"Wonderful! I was here once with my family, but it was a long time ago, and I was so small I remember almost nothing."

Jordan explained the history of the Bahamas, mentioning that the coves and secluded harbors had made it a popular area with pirates and buccaneers centuries before. Gina was about to mention her family's salvor business when Jordan drew her attention to another sight, and the thought slipped her mind.

Content to let Jordan make their plans for the day and set the pace, Gina and her handsome companion explored the picturesque waterfront. They stopped to watch vendors behind makeshift tables selling fresh fish and conch. The area

110

bustled with noisy activity as brightly clad natives, muscular and dark-skinned, cried commands in shrill tones and set about the process of unloading cargos from small inter-island vessels that came into port, laden with produce and goods from outer areas.

"The original Indian inhabitants called themselves *ceboynas*," Jordan explained. "Christopher Columbus was the first person to call them Indians. Probably because he mistakenly thought he'd landed in India. The Bahamians consider Columbus and his men their first tourists." Jordan grinned. "It seems they've been in the entertainment and tourism business ever since!"

A few blocks away Jordan hailed a surrey and helped Gina into the horse-drawn carriage. He settled in beside her, spoke to the driver, then relaxed and laid his arm across the back of the carriage seat as he pointed out landmarks with his free hand.

Jordan discharged the driver later when they came to the native market. Plump, local women in stalls lining the street had gathered to market their wares, woven of straw.

Gina picked through the brilliantly decorated handbags in a stall. "They're so pretty!" she exclaimed.

Jordan watched Gina's eyes and gauged her reactions to the various bags, until he had determined her favorite. He picked it up when she set it down and moved on.

"You must have this, Gina. No one—but no one—comes to Nassau without buying a souvenir made of straw. I'm getting you this bag. You can use it to carry other souvenirs back to the ship."

"Oh, but you can't!"

"Yes, I can," Jordan said flatly. In spite of Gina's protests, the native woman took the money and smiled with approval when Jordan turned to Gina and held the bag out to her. Gina hesitated and Jordan's eyes grew amused.

"Don't let old-fashioned ideas stop you," Jordan chided. "It's a simple, inexpensive handbag. Hardly a purchase that's going to compromise you. It was my suggestion you get a bag—and my gift to you. Please accept it without making a scene!"

Gina knew he meant what he said. He didn't intend to use the item later as some kind of leverage.

"Thank you. It's lovely and I'll always especially enjoy it because it's a gift from you . . ."

Jordan looked pleased at her words, but his voice was disparaging when he spoke. "Don't mention it. It's nothing."

Gina felt the sting of the cool words, spoiling the moment. She realized that the gift probably *was* nothing to Jordan! At that moment Gina realized she had been hoping that Jordan had enjoyed giving the handbag as much as she had enjoyed receiving it. But to him it was—"nothing." Not worth mentioning.

With all thoughts of Jordan pushed from her mind, Gina shopped for souvenirs, glad now that Jordan had insisted she have the bag, which neatly swallowed the many tokens she purchased to take to friends back in Bridgeton.

Jordan stood aside and watched with amusement while Gina discovered the unusual items at bargain prices and mentally composed a list of people to remember. Gina was so preoccupied with her own purchases that she scarcely noticed Jordan had bought no souvenirs.

After a traditional lunch of conch salad, Jordan suggested they return to the ship. As tired as Gina felt, and as sore as her feet were, she still hated to see the day end.

"You need to take your things to the ship and rest up for tonight when we come ashore again," Jordan explained.

Gina couldn't help the frown that slipped unbidden to her face. As much as she wanted to return with Jordan—she was annoyed by his assumption that she would! Gina felt both dismayed and pleased by his plans. But what about Hugh? Gina fretted that something unforeseen had come up. —that he might be ill.

"You don't like the idea?" Jordan asked, noticing the look of concern on Gina's face.

"It's not that. It's just that—"

Understanding lighted Jordan's eyes. "I'm sorry. I didn't stop to think you might already have made plans."

"No, I haven't."

"Then there's nothing standing in the way of your being with me . . . except your own choice. Is that it?"

Although Jordan's voice was carefully unconcerned, Gina sensed that her answer was important to him and that he was disturbed by the idea that she might not want to be with him.

"Nothing at all!" she said, with decisiveness. "And I will!"

A grin broke across Jordan's face and his eyes lightened like a patch of blue appearing from behind a dark cloud.

Gina let herself into her stateroom when Jordan saw her to her door and promised to stop by for her later. She was surprised to find Maureen there ahead of her. The pretty fashion consultant kicked off her shoes and wriggled her toes luxuriously.

"Back already?" Maureen's voice displayed her surprise. "I caught sight of Hugh going into a curio and pawnshop downtown. Roddy and I were on our way back to the ship, I didn't see you, but I thought you must be somewhere in the crowd."

"You didn't see me because I wasn't with Hugh."

"You weren't? But I thought you said you were going to see Nassau with him!"

"I thought so, too." Gina began packing away the

souvenirs. "I must have misunderstood Hugh. I'm sure I did."

"Oh, Gina! You didn't end up going ashore by yourself, did you?"

"I had company," Gina assured her.

"Anyone I know?"

"Jordan Gentry."

"You're kidding! You *didn't* go with him!"

"I'm not kidding. And, yes, I did! I didn't find Jordan as awful as Hugh claims he is. He was pleasant and polite. Not," Gina added quickly, "that I think Hugh lied about Jordan, but he was very courteous to me."

"So you spent the day with the infamous Jordan Gentry." Maureen's rich chuckle caused Gina to look up with a questioning glance. "No wonder Miss Moneybags was fit to be tied when I saw her milling around all by her lonesome. Danielle Elliot looked fit to kill, Gina, and I wondered what on earth could have put her in such a mood. Now I know!"

CHAPTER 10

GINA HAD FELT comfortable with Jordan all day but, as she slipped on a dress suitable for visiting night clubs, a sense of apprehension overwhelmed her. Maureen had already left with Roddy Tedrick when Jordan arrived at Gina's door. His coal black hair crested away from his tanned face and his clear blue eyes were intensified by the pale blue linen suit he wore.

Gina had dressed in a becoming flame-orange dress of a clingy material. Its full skirt and tapered bodice accentuated Gina's slim figure and highlighted her tawny coloring and russet hair. Jordan's eyes were frankly admiring.

Nassau by night was in sharp contrast with the city by day when the tropical sun beat down relentlessly, except where spreading palm fronds offered a cool haven. The first club rumbled with the primordial beat of the native music that contained heavy overtones of African tunes mingled with the throbbing, chanting calypso rhythm.

Again, at Jordan's suggestion, they dined on a traditional meal. Later, so Gina could sample most of what Nassau had to offer in a very short time, they club-hopped, staying only long enough for Gina to pick up the atmosphere and see the unusual sights before jumping into a taxi and off to the next exotic location.

Exhausted, Gina was relieved when Jordan suggested that they return to the *Tropical Star*. During the taxi ride to the waterfront, Gina's head drooped to Jordan's shoulder. She felt as if she were about to drop off to sleep when the driver halted and Jordan helped her from the cab.

Instead of turning toward the staterooms, Jordan took Gina's hand and led her to the upper deck. He was silent all the way. Gina studied his serious profile in the soft light. Jordan looked like a man with many thoughts pressing heavily on his mind.

Several times that night Gina had caught Jordan regarding her in a strange, brooding way, as if he were assessing the situation—and her. Gina sensed, even when he remained silent, that later he would broach the subject that had caused his thoughtful preoccupation all evening.

When they reached a lonely portion of the deck, Jordan leaned back against the railing. Gina looked up expectantly, waiting for him to speak. Instead, impulsively, as if he could not help himself, Jordan reached for her, and once again Gina was in his arms, his lips crushing her.

This time Gina knew that *she* had not moved to kiss *him!* She had not thrown herself at him. After the wonderful day with Jordan, his thoughtful attention, and the fond memories he had provided, Gina found herself returning his kiss. Moment by moment the emotions deepened. Jordan was pleased when Gina relaxed in his arms, and he murmured tender words of approval and encouragement. His embrace tightened until Gina was molded against him and his lips grew savage with possessiveness. Gina sensed Jordan was trying to hold back, to show restraint, but found it impossible. Gina's heart raced and her breath came in a syncopated rhythm.

"Gina . . . my darling Gina . . ."

Jordan released Gina an instant and stared down at her a long, hard moment before his strong fingers crept to her neck, traced the line of her jaw to cup her chin, then held her lips prisoner to his seeking mouth. Deep within, unfamiliar passions stirred and spread through her like molten lava. Gina knew she should pull away from Jordan's tantalizing embrace. But with his expert kisses and caresses, she no longer had any strength or will power. She swayed weakly against him. His breath was warm on her cheek as he pecked short, taunting kisses on her lips and whispered loving words, coaxing her to follow him down a path to sweet ecstacy.

At the suggestion, it was like a veil had been lifted from before her eyes. Like a sleepwalker awakening, she came to her senses, recoiling from the stark realization of what Jordan Gentry had asked! Gina wrestled out of his arms. Shocked by the sudden change in her demeanor, he released her. For a tortured minute neither of them spoke. Gina gripped the railing for the strength to keep from throwing herself back into Jordan's embrace.

He touched her shoulder. She flinched, yet drew pleasure from the contact. Then she shrugged his hand away. Jordan sighed with exasperation but he did not move to touch her further.

"Dont't be a tease!" he said, his voice walking a thin line between pleading and anger. "You want me. Gina. And I want you. We're adults, for crying out loud. Stop playing games. Be a woman for once, or quit leading me on only to turn and run like a silly child."

"You don't understand. Yes, I want you, but . . ."

Jordan cocked his eyebrow sarcastically and silenced

Gina. "I'm afraid I understand all too well. You want me, Gina, but you're afraid. Afraid, perhaps, of the woman you could become if you'd let yourself go. If you'd live a little! Admitting you want me is half the battle."

"Jordan, I don't like the turn this conversation is taking. Now, if you'll excuse me," Gina's voice was cold. She turned to brush past him. His hand snaked out and forced her to face him.

"Listen to me!" he snapped harshly. "I've wanted you since the moment we met. I've wanted you like I've never wanted any woman before. You want me, too. Don't bother to try to deny it now. No woman kisses a man like you kissed me if she doesn't have something in mind."

Gina was numbed by his insinuations. "I'm sorry you seem to have misunderstood . . ." she murmured miserably, as the world began to spin in a sickening manner. "I could never give what you seem to expect." Gina's voice shook with emotion, then cracked as tears forced their way near the surface. The wonderful day with Jordan was now permanently soiled by the revelation of his expectations.

"You *can!*" He said. "If you want to. I'll be honest with you, Gina. I want you—and I'll take you on whatever terms you give me. Whatever it is you want—I'll pay the price."

"Jordan!" Hot tears pooled in Gina's eyes.

"Don't be a fool. Everyone has a price, Gina, *everyone!* Even you!" Jordan's voice became bitingly cruel. "Name your price and I'll pay it. What is it you want from me?"

The hateful question rang in her ears even when Jordan ceased to speak further. Jordan's breathing was a harsh rasp in the still night.

She knew many people—good people—had their price. For some, it was money; for others, power; for others, prestige. She was stricken by Jordan's insinuation that she had a price, and to possess her was only a matter of finding the proper terms of barter!

Swallowing sobs, Gina turned away. Jordan's hand, encircling her wrist, spun her around to face him. His eyes were inches from hers.

"I want you . . ." Jordan reminded her in a hoarse voice. His mouth roughly claimed hers for his own once more. Gina squirmed. She scratched at his face, trying to free herself from his embrace, but Jordan seemed oblivious to her struggling.

Now, with Jordan's kiss, Gina's blood flowed like ice water through her veins. Revulsion boiled in the pit of her stomach. The only response Jordan gained from her was a trembling weakness—but it wasn't the trembling of desire. Powerful sobs wracked her shoulders and shook her body.

Shocked, Jordan released her. Unable to stop herself now that she was free, Gina raised her arm to slap his face—hard—as hard as she could. Instinctively, expecting the blow, Jordan parried to counter the motion. Realizing what she'd been about to do, Gina, her face bowed with tears, dropped her hand limply to her side.

"Oh, God . . ." Jordan murmured a half-prayer.

The agonized sound deep in his throat seemed to echo in the night. Gina didn't turn to look at him. And Jordan dared not make a move to go to her. He stared after her in wretched silence as Gina, blinded by tears, crept away. Only when she seemed about to disappear into the night and out of his life did he spring to action. This time he went after her. Touching her arm gently, he pleaded with her to stop, although he fully expected her to rebuff his touch.

"Gina, please. Stop and look at me. Just this one time is all I ask. Please! It's important."

The lost tone in Jordan's hollow, empty voice halted her. Slowly she faced him, drained, her eyes dull. It seemed that every time she allowed herself to trust Jordan Gentry, to become vulnerable by admitting her feelings for him, he only proved that his reputation was well deserved—he was an untrustworthy, heartless playboy!

"Gina, don't torment me. At least allow me the decency of apologizing to you."

Gina didn't know if she lifted her eyes to Jordan's under her own strength or if his fingers, incredibly strong, yet at times so tender, had touched her chin and tipped her face for her eyes to meet his.

"I'm sorry, Gina," he whispered. "Sorrier than you'll ever know. As God is my witness, I swear I don't know what possessed me to speak to you like that, to say the things I did. I had no right. I hope you can forgive me, but if you can't—I'll understand."

Gina was unable to look away from the despair in his sad eyes. "You're forgiven, Jordan. I accept your apology."

For an instant Jordan stared at Gina as if he couldn't believe her words. But the meaning in Gina's eyes revealed the truth. He had asked her to forgive him—and he had been forgiven. Just like that! Instantly. With Gina Roberts, forgiveness wasn't a pat ideology. It was a way of life.

"Thank you," he whispered contritely. "It was all my fault."

"No . . . we were probably both at fault," Gina murmured. "I'm sorry if I led you on. I didn't mean to."

"It's been a long day," Jordan wearily changed the subject. "Let me see you safely to your stateroom." He expected he might be brushed aside.

Gina was hesitant. "Well, if you'd like . . ."

Jordan walked with Gina to her room, pained by the awkward silence that hung between them. He realized there was little left to say that could bridge the gulf.

"Good night, Gina," he whispered, when she stopped at

her door. He sensed he might as easily have told her good-bye. But Gina gave him a shy, gentle smile that instantly kindled a spark of hope.

"Can I see you again?" Jordan managed the words even as he feared Gina's answer.

His heart seemed to stop beating as he waited for her decision. She dipped her head forward in a scarcely discernible nod.

"Yes," she whispered in a breeze-soft voice. Then, impulsively, Gina stood on tiptoe and brushed a kiss across Jordan's troubled cheek. She touched his shoulder with a friendly gesture, then she was gone.

Gina was unlike any woman he'd known. All his life women had been available—even those who had tried to signal they were not. Gina was different, so different it troubled him, confused him, and shook his masculine confidence to the core.

Despite what had happened, he still wanted to possess Gina. To love her. To know her body, soul, beliefs. It had been his own raging desires that had caused him to act like a brute. When he saw what he'd done to her, and witnessed gentle Gina, broken, crying, so very hurt, he wanted only to soothe away her tears and protect her from the hurt he himself had inflicted.

At that moment Jordan had wanted to touch Gina with understanding instead of ravish her with desire. He dared not move. He knew within that he wanted not only to possess Gina Roberts . . . he wanted to marry her!

Marriage! The idea was tantalizing. Marriage had never been an option he had seriously considered. He felt he wasn't the marrying kind. Now he began to wonder. And worry. If he married Gina, would she make him unbearably happy for a short while? And then, when the passion had waned, would he make Gina wretchedly miserable for a lifetime?

121

Troubled thoughts kept Jordan awake throughout the night. The sun was bursting above the horizon when he finally sank into heavy sleep. All day long Jordan slept, while the cruise ship steamed toward their next stop, Port-au-Prince. By the time he awakened—later that evening—he felt groggy. With effort he shaved and dressed. Leaving his stateroom, he looked for Gina, but she was nowhere in sight. Then, miraculously, Danielle Elliot was beside him almost before he gave conscious thought to seeking her out.

Gina expected that, after Jordan's apology, she would probably see him the next day. When he did not appear, Gina was quick to accept Hugh's invitation to tour Port-au-Prince. This time she knew the plans were solid—not a slipshod assumption on her part.

Maureen was up and about when Hugh and Gina returned from breakfast to prepare to go ashore. The atmosphere of the ship was charged with excitement as they entered the harbor of Port-au-Prince, the capital of the island of Haiti.

A half hour later Hugh and Gina were among the first to go ashore aboard the small shuttle. Hugh, who'd been on Caribbean cruises in the past, knew his way around the familiar port. Gina was fascinated by the plush hotels, elegant restaurants, and many art galleries in the city.

Native boutiques and marketplaces teemed with people—a colorful montage of sights and sounds, mingled with the fragrance of the exquisite tropical flowers.

Downtown Port-au-Prince proved to be a panorama of small children hawking *frescos,* ices with syrup. Young girls roasted ears of corn on outdoor grills. Beggars jostled in the streets, stirring Gina's pity. Gaily painted passenger jitneys wove through the busy streets. The Iron Market was composed of stalls with everything from fruit and fabric to voodoo drums and love potions.

After a luncheon of Rice Dion-Dion, a mixture of black Haitian mushrooms and rice, Hugh suggested they escape the blistering heat and return to the ship to rest up for the evening.

"I'll be waiting," Gina promised.

Gina slipped off her shoes and picked up a book. Curling up on the bed, she considered taking a nap. Instead, she lay awake thinking about Hugh. More and more Gina feared that she had come to mean more to Hugh than he would ever mean to her. Gina valued Hugh as a friend, but she sensed Hugh wanted more from her than friendship.

"Maybe if I buy you a bottle of love potion," Hugh had teased as he held up a small bottle of wickedly black liquid, "then you'll fall in love with me!"

Gina placed love potions in the same category with voodoo charms, lucky numbers, and horoscopes. She passed them off with the confidence of a believer who knows God controls her destiny.

"Not a chance, Hugh!"

Gina blurted the words before she realized the hurt they would cause Hugh. She had meant that it would take God—not a potion—to inspire love in her heart. But Hugh looked as if she had slapped his face with her cold, unfeeling words.

Gina considered trying to explain her words, then decided not to take a chance on deepening the hurt Hugh already felt. Gina said nothing and was relieved when Hugh blandly drew her attention to a display of small curios.

When Hugh wandered away to look over some jewelry, Gina picked through souvenirs and made a few purchases. When they left for the ship, Hugh held out a small sack.

"This is for you."

"For me?" Gina looked at Hugh and saw a shy smile lingering near his lips.

"For none other," Hugh said airily. "I saw it. It reminded me of you. So I bought it."

"Hugh, you shouldn't have . . ."

"Don't say that before you've seen it."

When Gina upturned the sack, a small, delicate necklace dropped into the palm of her hand. Her eyes flew to meet Hugh's proud gaze.

"It's beautiful!—but much too expensive!"

Hugh waved away her words. "To me the price is small. Just a trinket—but a pretty one. I wanted you to have it so that somewhere, someday, you'll look at it and remember the good times we've had . . . no matter what happens between us."

Gina looked into Hugh's kindly brown eyes and felt a rush of affection. Impulsively she kissed his cheek and took his hand as they strolled down the street.

"I'll always remember the good times, Hugh. You know that. I love the necklace. If I'd seen it myself, I'd have bought it."

"Let me put it on for you."

Hugh took the necklace from Gina and admired the cross with the Lord's Prayer etched in tiny letters on the back. Gina stood motionless as Hugh clicked the clasp in place. Then unable to restrain himself, he dropped a light kiss to the downy nape of her neck before turning her to face him so he could admire the gold cross at her throat.

Back in her room Gina looked at the necklace. She knew her feelings for Hugh were confusing, but she had faith in the words Christ had taught his followers to use when praying to the Father. Gina trusted with all her heart that if she had faith in the Lord He would reveal His will so it could be done on earth as it was in heaven.

Gina gradually grew drowsy and fell asleep. She was unsure how long she had napped when a thudding noise on her door aroused her. Startled, she looked at her watch, afraid that Hugh had arrived early to find her not yet ready. Instead Gina opened the door to stare into Jordan Gentry's unfathomable eyes. Sleepily she blinked at him.

"What do you want?" Gina spoke before she could censor the sound of her words.

Jordan's lips quirked in a dry smile. "What I want is to ask you to go ashore with me tonight. I haven't seen you in two days."

"Your fault, not mine. I'm sorry, but I already have other plans."

Slowly the drowsiness cleared from Gina's head as Jordan stood by in silence, and she wondered if he had the audacity to expect her to change her plans. Then she decided he was simply reluctant to leave.

"If you have other plans, then I guess that means I'll have to make other plans too."

Without another word, he left. Gina closed the door after him, feeling an unpleasant mixture of relief and disappointment. What right did he have to come to her stateroom after almost two days' absence and assume she'd be ready and waiting? Worse, it seemed that he had been threatening her with the casual reference to his "other plans."

Gina was about to wrestle again with the thorny questions Jordan's behavior had raised when Hugh arrived. His companionship was a pleasant diversion from her troubled thoughts.

After dinner Gina and Hugh left the restaurant and walked through the city. Throughout the streets coal braziers, usually improvised from old auto fenders, had been set up by industrious women cooking *grillots*, grilled pork, to be sold to passersby. The curbside vendors were in striking contrast to the rows of elegant restaurants reputed to be among the finest in the Caribbean.

Gina and Hugh sampled the atmosphere at several night clubs that were replete with colorfully costumed native dancers who were writhing to the hypnotic beat of the music and drums.

During the evening, without really being conscious of the fact, Gina scanned the crowds in the hope of catching a glimpse of Jordan. Though he was nowhere in sight—Danielle Elliot was, accompanied by a handsome auburn-haired man. Hugh and Gina met the pair as they entered a club together. Hugh nodded pleasantly.

"If looks could kill, love, you'd be on your way to Glory!" Hugh murmured to Gina.

"I wonder what's wrong with her?" Gina fretted.

"Who knows?" Hugh shrugged. "And who cares?"

Gina laughed with him, but in her heart, Gina found she did care. She had done nothing to deserve the hostile glances the blonde gave her every time they met. There was only one reason that could account for Danielle's hatred—Jordan Gentry!

But that didn't make sense! Gina had been with Jordan only in Nassau. Since then she had been seen exclusively with Hugh. Danielle had no basis for her anger.

Gina had assumed Jordan would be seeing the port city with Danielle. She was surprised to learn it was not so. Idly, Gina wondered who Jordan was with, venturing a guess that he was hardly spending his evening alone. Not with so many attractive women available for the asking.

But Jordan Gentry *was* alone.

After learning that Gina's plans didn't include him, he returned to his room. Jordan had seen the port so many times it no longer held any special attraction for him. He preferred, instead, to remain secluded in his room and think his thoughts about Gina, his future, and the purpose behind his life.

For two days he hadn't seen Gina. At first it was only because he had overslept. The next day he avoided her on purpose. Now, after seeing her just once, he knew he had to be with Gina at any cost. The times he'd spent with the lovely girl since the *Tropical Star* sailed were among the happiest in recent years. Jordan decided he would live for the moment and draw what pleasure he could from her company, and willingly face a bleak future without her when the time came.

Jordan had plotted ways to avoid being thrown into contact with Gina. Now he began to examine strategies that would ensure a meeting with Gina.

Knowing her habits, and that she was an early riser, Jordan took breakfast when he suspected Gina would be in the dining room. To his relief she was present and Hugh was not. When Jordan approached her table, Gina politely invited him to join her.

While they made small talk, Jordan noticed the way Gina's eyes occasionally roved toward the door as if waiting for Hugh to arrive. When he did not, and Gina prepared to leave, so did Jordan.

"What are your plans for today?" Jordan asked.

"I haven't taken time to make any."

Jordan gave her a grin. "Do you have any objections to spending some time with me?"

Gina regarded him, detecting the hope in his eyes and in his voice.

"I . . . but . . ." Gina fumbled for words, not wanting to hurt either Jordan or Hugh.

"I won't force my company on you. Not if there's something—or someone—you'd rather be with. Is there?"

"No. The day's yours, if you like."

The day with Jordan was splendid. The time passed much too quickly. It was a great deal later when Jordan walked her to her stateroom. Outside her door he kissed her—but very differently this time. There was tenderness and respect in the gentle brush of his lips on hers. Surprisingly Gina hungered for more of them.

Abruptly Jordan released her and smiled down at her before dropping one last careless kiss on the tip of her pert nose.

"Same time, same place tomorrow?" he asked. "We can see Kingston together."

"It's a date."

Jordan was waiting when Gina arrived for breakfast. She'd just been seated when Hugh appeared in the room. Seeing her, he took a few tentative steps in her direction before he recognized Jordan. His steps froze. Gina forced a smile and waved him toward them. Curtly he shook his head, turned, and left.

Jordan went on with their conversation as if nothing had happened, but Gina's responses were automatic and uninspired. She ached when she recalled the sharp look of disappointment in Hugh's eyes. Gina knew that Hugh would not have been content to be the extra man at her table. She knew, too, that he must be disturbed to discover that she had chosen Jordan's company over his own. The hurt in Hugh's eyes blighted Gina's day even though Jordan took special pains to make the port stop a memorable one for her.

That night when Jordan walked Gina to her stateroom, she felt a sense of keen relief when he didn't set up plans for another day together. Gina wanted to see Hugh to be sure he didn't feel she no longer cared for him.

The next morning neither Hugh nor Jordan were in the dining room when Gina ate a quick breakfast with several other passengers before returning to her stateroom. Her roommate, dressed for the sun, was brushing her luxuriant hair.

128

"What are you doing today?" Maureen asked.

"I thought I'd go swimming this morning."

"Care if I tag along?"

"I'd love it."

At the pool Maureen dabbed on tanning oil before reclining in a chaise to face the sun.

"I thought you were going swimming," Gina remarked and slipped into the pool.

Maureen raised her head and smiled, squinting against the sun. "First I'm going to soak up some sun, Paleface. Maybe later."

Gina was not aware of Jordan's presence until he dived cleanly into the pool and surfaced beside her. Jordan's eyes skimmed appreciatively over her neat figure revealed in the wet swimming suit.

"Gina!" Maureen called. "Wake me up if I fall asleep, okay? I doze off every time I try to tan and forget to turn over."

Gina nodded and swam beside Jordan. Several children were splashing in the pool but, when their interest waned, Jordan and Gina had the area to themselves.

"It must be about time to wake your sleeping friend and tell her to toast the other side," Jordan reminded her.

"I will in another minute or two if she doesn't wake up on her own."

"You swim well," Jordan commented. "Especially for a girl from the North. Surely the lakes are frozen half the year and there are not too many indoor pools."

"You swim expertly yourself," Gina observed. "And you're a terrific diver."

Jordan grinned and flicked water from his tanned face. "I should be," he said in a matter-of-fact voice. "When I was in the Navy I was a frogman. That's when I learned to dive. It was my life then and I made it my living for a few years after I mustered out of the Navy. I dived for a salvage operation.''

"You did?'' Gina cried. She was about to tell Jordan about the Roberts' family business. Just then Maureen awakened and looked at the watch that she'd tucked into her sandal.

"Who's sleeping on the job, Gina!'' Maureen called. "You were supposed to wake me up!''

"I was on my way. I was going to wake you up—like this!'' Gina cupped her hand and sent a spray of water cascading to Maureen's sun-baked skin.

The tall brunette bolted upright with a jerk. "Regina Anne Roberts! I'll get you for that!''

"Try it, Maureen,'' Gina taunted. "Come on in—the water's fine!'' In answer Maureen stuck out her tongue and rolled over in the sun. "Who did you dive for?'' Gina asked, turning back to Jordan. "My family has a salvor ship in the Caribbean. I lived on the ship when I was small and met some of the other salvors, Dad seemed to know them all. Maybe I know the people you dived for.''

"What?'' Jordan's whisper was distant as if he hadn't heard a word Gina had spoken.

"I asked the name of the company you dived for.''

"No one,'' he said in a soft, curt voice. "No one you'd know.''

"Oh. Well . . . I thought . . .'' Gina's words died an uncomfortable death on her lips.

From the peculiar look that swept across Jordan's features, it was obvious that he wanted to end the discussion. But why? Gina could only wonder. Quickly, almost rudely, Jordan turned his back on her, executed a shallow surface dive, swam underwater to the ladder, climbed out, slung a fluffy towel around his neck, and headed for his room.

What had she done now? Gina stared after him. What on

earth could she have said to have caused such an instantaneous change?

"What's eating *him?*" Maureen asked, speaking Gina's thoughts. "He left as if the Devil were after him!"

"I don't know," Gina said. Her voice shook, then steadied in resolve. She was tired of Jordan Gentry. Tired of his off-again, on-again ways. "I don't know what's wrong with him—and furthermore—I don't care!"

But in her heart Gina knew that no matter how often or how vigorously she denied it, the truth was that she *did* care—very, very much. Otherwise, Jordan could not hurt her with such ease.

CHAPTER 11

JORDAN SLAMMED THE DOOR of his stateroom after him and saw his own eyes in the ashen reflection that stared back from the mirror. Jordan realized he'd just handled the situation poorly—but his first instinct had been to cut and run. He flopped onto the bed, unmindful of his wet trunks, and the blood pounded in his temples, along with the words that shrieked unmercifully in his mind. Maureen's words:

"Regina Anne Roberts! I'll get you for that!"

Why, oh why, hadn't he figured it out before?

There were many families named Roberts, of course, but he should have given some thought to Luke Roberts when he met another person with the same last name. He hadn't—not for a moment—not even when the attractive woman looked so hauntingly familiar that he truly believed he knew her.

Jordan *had* known Gina from another place and time. Though she was honest in assuring him that they had never met, Jordan had seen countless snapshots of the young Gina tacked up aboard the *Sea Nymph*. Luke and Gerald doted on the girl—Reggie. The woman Jordan knew as . . . Gina!

Jordan cursed himself and his luck for not making the connection. How was he to guess that the beautiful woman, the woman who filled his dreams, was his best friend's little sister?

With this new information, Jordan realized he couldn't take the chance of lingering around Gina, intent on enjoying her company. Given his volatile temperament, he feared that her nearness would, at some time, provide an irresistible opportunity for seduction. But the memory of Gerald and the friendship of Luke Roberts demanded he protect her virtue and preserve his honor.

Jordan knew now that, without question, Gina Roberts wasn't a woman who would betray her faith for anything or anyone. Her faith was the legacy passed on to her by a loving, Christian family. Jordan felt the earthy temptations that had mingled with his admiration of Gina slip away to be replaced by a deeper consideration and respect.

A few nights before, Jordan had turned his back on Gina for his own peace of mind—so she wouldn't interfere with the worldly existence he found so comfortable. This time Jordan would not avoid Gina for *his* sake—he would do it for *her* sake. For Luke's. Jordan realized he loved Gina more than he'd ever loved another woman. He cared enough about her to leave her alone!

The remainder of the day was a lonely one for Gina. She had grown accustomed to Jordan's presence filling her hours. Without him, and without Hugh, time dragged by with dull monotony. Maureen invited Gina to join her and Roddy Tedrick, the brother of an old college friend, but Gina declined the offer.

"Thanks, but I'll find something to do. Don't worry about me."

That night Gina dined alone, with every intention of returning to her stateroom to read. On her way out of the dining room, she met Hugh, who was also sitting alone. At the sight of her, his eyes glowed with such delight that Gina felt shamed for having ignored him in past days.

"It's nice seeing you again, Gina."

"It's good to see you, too, Hugh."

Their conversation was strained and stilted. Gina waited for the words that would translate to mean "I-told-you-so," even when she knew Hugh would not speak them. For an odd moment Gina suspected she would have felt better if he had!

"What's on your docket for tonight?" Hugh asked.

"Nothing . . . yet."

Hugh gave Gina a curt look. "Is that an acceptance to my unspoken invitation?"

"If that's a backhanded invitation to spend some time with you tonight—the answer is yes. I've missed you, Hugh."

"And I've missed you." Hugh's voice became soft and faraway. Instead of going to a lounge, they strolled the decks. "I've done more than just miss you, Gina. I've felt almost wild without you. Lost." Hugh raised his eyes to hers. "But I wasn't going to intrude—I don't go where I'm not wanted. I've never thought of myself as a jealous man. But seeing you with Jordan . . ." Hugh shrugged, unable to continue.

"Hugh—I know."

"No, you *don't* know," he said almost fiercely. "You can't! Seeing you with Jordan proved to me that you're not just another pretty girl. It made me realize how much I love you. Seeing you with another man—with Jordan—when I love and want you so much was almost more than I could take."

"I didn't mean to hurt you, Hugh. I would never do that. I've suspected how you felt."

"But you, Gina. How do *you* feel?"

Gina met Hugh's intent eyes and detected his hope as he waited for her to say the words Gina knew she could not utter. Hugh wanted her to say them—he needed to hear them—but Gina couldn't tell Hugh she loved him.

"I don't know how I feel." Gina searched for the right words. "I know that I like you very much. I'm fonder of you than I had imagined." Gina faced him squarely and her eyes held questions. "Hugh, I don't know. I really don't know."

Hugh sighed and took Gina in his arms. "I want to marry you, Gina," Hugh murmured. "I love you! I was hoping you loved me, too."

"Hugh, I'm touched. But the way I feel now—so confused—so uncertain—I couldn't marry you or any man. Not when I don't know my own heart. When I marry, it will have to be for love alone."

Hugh released her and took Gina's hand. "I understand," he comforted. "That's why you're a woman worth waiting for. To some, love comes slowly, softly. For me, love came quickly. I long for the day when you'll feel as I do. As long as I know there's hope for me, Gina, that I have a chance with you . . ."

"If you're the man for me, God will reveal it to my heart. Then I'll know."

Hugh nodded his acceptance. "Until that day I'll be patient. But try not to let pretty daydreams steal reality and true love away from you. That's all I ask."

That night Gina thought about her relationship with Hugh. She knew she didn't love him. She couldn't love Hugh when her heart belonged to Jordan Gentry!

"Gina! Gina! Guess what?" Maureen burst into the

135

stateroom and plopped down on the bed, hugging herself.

"Brent's flying to San Juan! I just got the message. He says he misses me and he's going to fly in for the weekend we're in port. Isn't that fantastic?"

"Wonderful! You're going to have a terrific time!"

"Just seeing Brent will be heaven," Maureen said. "It's only been a few days, but, sometimes, Gina, it seems like a century since I saw him. I can hardly wait!"

"You won't have to for very long. We see Santa Domingo tomorrow and then sail for San Juan."

"You're seeing the port with Hugh?" Maureen questioned. Gina noticed how carefully Maureen avoided mentioning Jordan.

Gina nodded. "That's what we have planned."

Maureen smiled. "He looked so happy with you at his side, Gina. It was as if Hugh realized he had the world on a string. He loves you—doesn't he?"

"That's what he says."

Maureen caught the note of uncertainty. "And you? How do you feel?"

"I like him," Gina said frankly. "But it's not love. At least, I don't think it is."

"If you don't know—then it's not love," Maureen asserted. "When it's love—the real thing—believe me, you'll know!"

The next morning Gina toured Santa Domingo with Hugh. The city extended for miles in every direction. They explored the beautifully restored Old City where Gina bought some inexpensive jewelry, crafted from local gems, to take back to friends.

In the evening the couple dined in a small restaurant, before strolling to a quiet piano bar where they could talk. From the corner of her eye Gina caught sight of Jordan Gentry arm-in-arm with Danielle Elliot. Before Gina's eyes

136

they laughingly made their way across the street into a disco that pulsated with the music of a hard, driving beat.

Both Hugh and Gina pretended they hadn't seen the handsome couple. But, with Jordan on her mind again, the conversation took a decided downturn.

The next day was a torment. The less Gina saw of Jordan, the more her eyes roved the crowds, straining for a glimpse of him. The more she tried to content herself with Hugh's companionship, the more she longed to be with Jordan.

On Friday morning, when the luxury liner slipped into port in San Juan, Brent was waiting for Maureen.

"Come see Brent," Maureen begged Gina and Hugh. "You've got to meet him, Hugh!"

The two followed Maureen through the crowd to where Brent waited. Maureen flung herself into his arms and covered his face with kisses. Brent hugged her happily before he turned to Gina and Hugh.

"Would you care to join us for the day?" Brent asked after Maureen had made the introductions.

"No, I wouldn't dream of intruding on your weekend!" Hugh said. "Maybe we'll see you later."

Gina found the capital city of Puerto Rico very American. As modern as it appeared in many ways, it seemed incredible to learn that San Juan is one of the oldest cities in the Western hemisphere.

The couple made their way through old San Juan, taking in the sights and sounds of the inviting, tree-lined streets, still paved with the original blue-glazed blocks brought over as ballast in the old Spanish sailing ships that ventured to the New World. Pastel-colored houses and structures were decorated with wrought-iron grillwork that served the functional purpose of protecting property and privacy.

In spite of the aggressive North American business atmosphere that was familiar to Gina, she noticed a foreign flavor in the Spanish spoken on all sides. Street vendors carried their wares in little carts or on their heads. The whistle of scissors-grinders pierced the air, and the noisy clanging triangle of the ice-cream vendor jangled gaily.

There was so much to see in the old city that Gina and Hugh decided to take their time over the weekend. After a leisurely lunch that provided them time to rest, they struck out to browse in the native shops and stalls. In one small shop Gina noticed Hugh admiring some exquisitely crafted bracelets of gold and silver.

"They're beautiful!" Gina exclaimed.

Hugh glanced at her. "Would you like to have one?" His eyes held a teasing glint.

"Not really," Gina said quickly, knowing that with the least show of interest Hugh would buy her any item she desired.

"I'd like to get you one, anyway," Hugh insisted. "Maybe I should get an *esclave* bracelet and keep it for good luck. We could end up fulfilling the legend."

"Legend?"

In halting English the shopkeeper explained the custom. *Esclave* bracelets—slave bracelets—were bands of precious metal given to a loved one.

"You add one band for each year of marriage," he said. He beamed at Gina. "Then, for each child that blesses the marriage, there is an etched band." Gina felt Hugh's eyes on her face, waiting, watching, reading her expression.

"I-I didn't know about the legend," she said weakly. Gina turned away, shaken. Hugh never really pressed her to marry him, but always, always the thought never seemed far from his mind!

Hugh winked at Gina and selected a silver band. He reached for his wallet. "I hate to disappoint the man," he whispered. "We'll get one—just in case." A weak smile rested on Gina's lips. "Who knows? Perhaps in future years, Gina, we'll come back to get more—one for each year—if it's meant to be."

Gina was exhausted, physically and emotionally, when she and Hugh arrived back at the ship. She was hoping for a quiet moment alone, but Maureen was dressing to go out to dinner with Brent.

"Back already? What did you buy, Gina?"

"Very little. Hugh bought a . . ." Gina started to tell Maureen about the slave bracelet, thought better of it, and decided it really wasn't worth mentioning. Maureen seemed preoccupied anyway.

"Did you have a nice time?"

"Pleasant enough."

"What plans have you made for tomorrow?" Maureen glanced into the mirror as she applied eyeshadow and watched for Gina's reply.

"We plan to visit the places we missed today."

"Does that include tomorrow night?" Maureen's voice held hope.

"What are you driving at?" Gina finally asked. "Out with it! There's no sense beating around the bush with me."

Maureen grinned. "You're right. I've got a problem and I need you to do me a favor. Will you?"

"Sure—if I can."

Maureen rolled her eyes. "You're the *only* one who can. I got myself into this pickle, but you've got to get me out. Brent asked about some of the people on the cruise, so I named some of the passengers I'd met. When I mentioned that Jordan was on board, Brent asked me to arrange a business date. He and Jordan not only know each other, but Jordan is in the process of expanding his company and is doing business with one of the Hamiltons' New York banks. Brent wanted to mix business and pleasure this weekend."

139

"I don't see how that should cause a problem. I'm sure you can arrange things."

"Arranging it was a snap," Maureen admitted. "Jordan agreed right away to meet with Brent. I let him know, in a nice way, that Danielle wasn't included in our plans."

"I still don't see your problem."

"My problem, Gina, is that Jordan assumes we have a dinner companion for him to round out the foursome—but I don't. Not unless you'll agree to come. Will you? Please? I couldn't bear the thought of an evening spent listening to Danielle Elliot's stupid, self-centered chatter!"

"I don't know. Don't you know someone else you can ask?"

Maureen shook her head. "I've been counting on you. Hugh won't mind. It's only for one night. You can tell him you're doing it as a favor to Brent. That's true enough."

"Oh, all right. I'll help you out," Gina agreed. Her voice held a degree of reluctance she didn't really feel at the prospect of being Jordan's dinner companion.

"Make sure you don't forget."

"I'll be there."

When Maureen turned back to the mirror, Gina caught the small, satisfied smile that flitted across the brunette's features. She began to view the situation with suspicion. Was the dinner really related to Brent's business? Or was Maureen making Gina's love life her concern? She frowned . . .

The next day Gina told Hugh she had made plans to go out with Brent, Maureen, and a business client. Hugh was affable and promised to make his own plans for the evening.

As the two girls prepared for the occasion, Maureen watched with approval as Gina selected a flame-colored dress that dropped to a deep V at the neckline and swirled outward from the nipped-in waist to fall in graceful folds about her knees. The warm hue complemented her skin, burnished from the sun, and ignited golden highlights in her hair.

By the time Brent arrived, Gina had never looked lovelier. Even Maureen commented on her radiance, and Brent gave a low whistle of appreciation as he offered an elbow to each of the beautiful young women.

When the maitre d' led them to the table Brent had reserved, Gina felt a sweep of nervousness. How would Jordan react when he discovered that she was his dinner companion? What if he turned on his heel and departed without a word as he had at the pool? It was too late to worry, she realized, when Jordan appeared and spoke to the maitre d'. The moment of truth was at hand.

"Good to see you again, Jordan." The younger banker arose and shook the tall businessman's hand before he motioned him to be seated at the table. "You already know Gina and Maureen." Jordan nodded greetings.

"A pleasant surprise, Gina."

From Jordan's tone of voice, Gina wasn't sure if his words were sincere or merely a facetious remark. As the conversation progressed, Gina relaxed in the knowledge that he was genuinely pleased to see her.

The bitter days of separation melted away and, in spite of her better judgment, Gina felt her hesitations regarding Jordan disappear, leaving her trusting heart vulnerable once more.

"Things are going well, don't you think?" Maureen asked when she and Gina excused themselves to freshen up. Maureen touched a puff to her nose. "You and Jordan make a handsome couple. And, even though I know he's been moody, I think he likes you very much."

"I had thought so a few times," Gina sighed. "But just

141

when it seemed that Jordan cared—something would happen to change it all.''

"I know what you mean," Maureen said. She touched Gina's arm with a sympathetic gesture. "Maybe it will all work out differently this time. There's not much time left."

If Gina had been intent on making Jordan Gentry fall in love with her, she knew she should be frantic with worry that she would not accomplish the deed in the few days left to her. But Gina was not apprehensive. If Jordan were not the man for her—no extended number of days, no amount of arranging, no special efforts—could make him love her. Ier destiny was not in her own hands—it rested in His. Even so, Gina gazed wistfully across the candlelight at Jordan—so handsome, so charming, so pleasant—and dreamed of what might be.

"Have you two settled the problems of the financial world?" Maureen asked gaily.

"Every business problem is settled, but that leaves us with a new problem. What do we do now?"

"Simple!" Maureen said smugly. "Brent, you're going to take me dancing. And Jordan, I'm sure you can find a way to show Gina such a lovely time she'll always have fond memories of old San Juan."

Gina's mouth dropped open. She'd come with Brent and Maureen. It hardly seemed decent for Maureen to foist her off on Jordan as if she assumed he had no later plans of his own.

"Maureen worked that neatly enough," Jordan mused when Brent and Maureen left them before Gina could find words, and before Jordan could smoothly extricate himself from the situation. "I'll bet she runs an efficient business."

"Maureen is an organizer," Gina agreed. "Just because she's good at arranging things—don't think you're obligated to go along with it, Jordan. I can find my own way back to the *Tropical Star* if you've something else you want to do."

"You're not going back to the liner—until you go back with me. The night is young and there's nothing I want more than to be with you." Jordan looked into Gina's amber eyes. "Strange as this may sound, Gina, I hope you'll understand how much I've missed you these past days."

Gina gave Jordan a playful look to hide the intensity of her deep feelings. "Funny, you could've fooled me!"

"I didn't have to fool you, Gina, because I was too busy fooling myself. I tried to tell myself I didn't care about you. I tried to convince myself I didn't miss you. And, I did a good job of it, too, until I saw you sitting there with Brent and Maureen. The past few days I've felt like half a person—tonight you made me feel whole again."

"Jordan, don't say something you don't mean," Gina begged and looked away. "Please don't."

"I *do* mean those things, Gina," he said fervently. "I've never meant anything more. Since knowing you I've felt as if I were being pulled in a dozen different directions. But always I was drawn back to you." Gina's heart fluttered at the intensity of his words. He sounded so sincere. When Jordan pulled her into his arms on the busy street, she felt dizzy with joy. "Gina, I love you . . . love you . . . love you . . ."

When his lips touched hers, she was in ecstasy. Secure in Jordan's arms, firm in his newly declared love, she wanted the night never to end, the adoration in Jordan's eyes never to leave.

Back at the *Tropical Star* they strolled hand-in-hand, enjoying the fresh ocean breezes. Trustingly Gina reveled in Jordan's strong arms when he swept her into his embrace. A happy sigh escaped him as Gina's lips yielded pliantly to his. Gina was aware of nothing—nothing but her love for the man she held in her arms—and wanted for her own. She was unaware of the soft waves slapping against the hull—of the faint throb of tropical music that cried far away in the night—of the soft, determined footsteps approaching . . .

"Well! If this isn't cute and cozy!" An angry voice pierced the silent night. Gina froze in Jordan's embrace. When she tried to pull free, not understanding, he restrained her. Then, together, Jordan and Gina turned to stare in shocked unison at the brutal intrusion. Danielle Elliot glowered back.

Her voice dripped with sarcasm. "So this is your important little business meeting, is it?" Her voice shook with fury. "It was all lies! You didn't have a business meeting." Danielle's shrill voice choked as she gasped for breath. "All you wanted was an excuse to be with . . . *her!* Someday, Jordan Gentry, when you're busy trying to decide which one of us you really want, you're going to discover you no longer have a choice! I won't play second fiddle to any woman—especially not to someone like Regina Roberts!"

Incredulously Gina looked from Jordan to Danielle, then back to Jordan. A kaleidoscope of emotions flashed over his lean features. Jordan appeared deceptively calm, but Gina sensed it was merely the eye of the storm which was gathering.

"That's enough, Danielle! I don't have to explain my whereabouts to you. If you want to think it's a lie—believe whatever you want."

Danielle coughed out a wet sob. Her face crumpled into angry tears. "Maybe I don't have a right to question your comings-and-goings, but I think Gina might find it interesting to know what a juggler you are, Jordan, trying to handle two love affairs at once!"

144

Jordan's voice remained controlled while Danielle vented her fury. The night which had been so perfect only minutes before now seemed shabby and shameful. No matter what Gina felt for Danielle as a person, she sensed the girl spoke the truth. Jordan *had* been with Danielle many times. And from what Hugh said, Gina knew that as far as Jordan was concerned, the woman he loved was the one he happened to be with at the moment.

Quickly, before Jordan could stop her, Gina turned and fled to her room. Jordan started after her, but Danielle clutched his arm and spun him back to face her wrath. The bitter argument raged. Gina covered her ears as she ran to her room, fighting for breath as she forced back hot tears, hoping they wouldn't fall until she was alone in her room.

Blessedly Maureen was still out with Brent when Gina fell sobbing to her bed. Only a few short hours before, she had been the happiest woman on earth. Now she believed she was the most miserable.

Gina had told Jordan she loved him. In her heart she knew it was true. But her love for Jordan was a wasted, worthless, foolish human emotion. Hugh, sensible Hugh, was right! Even if Jordan loved her, it would never work out. Never! Always she would live with the fear that some-day some woman would tempt Jordan to break any com-mitment he might ever give.

What she and Jordan had was only a facsimile of love. She knew it wasn't that perfect love for which she yearned, because the bond of the Lord was missing. Jordan offered her the only kind of love such a man could give. But Gina knew she had to hold out for more.

CHAPTER 12

GINA SPENT A RESTLESS night, locked in troubled sleep. Her dreams taunted her with slow-motion scenes of Jordan and Danielle. Dawn came and Gina awakened, more exhausted than before she had fallen across her bed.

Maureen was sleeping, so Gina dressed quietly and went for breakfast. Hugh was absent, and Gina was grateful to be able to sip her hot coffee in silence without having to explain her tear-reddened eyes.

Gina had left without giving Jordan a chance to explain. He had pleaded with her to wait. She was haunted now by the loving concern in his voice. But he had not followed her. He had chosen instead to remain with Danielle. No. The agony she was experiencing must be her own personal testing. Gina believed God was asking her to make a decision—one of the biggest in her life—Him . . . or Jordan Gentry. To Gina there was only one answer. She couldn't betray the Lord. Not for anyone. Not even for a man like Jordan.

Even though Gina sensed she'd made the right decision,

her heart continued to ache with heavy pain that eased only slightly when she dwelt on the knowledge that her faith would provide the strength she needed to face each day without Jordan.

Abrupt high-heeled steps clattering across the dining room jarred Gina from her thoughts. Startled, she stared directly into Danielle Elliot's icy blue gaze. The cruel light that gleamed there was frightening.

Danielle stopped short at Gina's table, unmindful of the diners who turned to observe. She glared down at Gina, then, without bothering to ask permission, jerked out the chair and sat down, intent on a showdown. Gina took a deep breath and faced Danielle squarely.

"What do you want?"

Danielle formed her words with terse lips and clipped speech. "What I want is for you to stay away from Jordan!" Danielle delivered the edict with a murderous glare. Her blue eyes bored into Gina's. "Stay away from him and out of my way or you'll be very, very sorry," she intoned in a solemn voice.

"You can't be serious! Danielle, you can hardly go around asking adults to do your bidding and expect them to obey."

"I'm not *asking* you, Gina. I'm *telling* you!" Danielle spat the words. With a stiff, marionette movement, she flung her hair away from her tear-swollen face.

"What if I don't go along with you?" Gina asked, no longer caring if she baited the angry woman further.

Danielle's eyes narrowed into slits. "If you don't, you'll be sorry. I'll see to that. Somehow." Danielle's chin was stony. The only crack in her veneer was the angry quiver of her lips. Her blue eyes flashed with determination. She looked away from Gina and furtively swiped at tears with the back of her hand.

"It's not fair!" Danielle whimpered, almost as much to herself as to Gina. "Sometimes you're all Jordan talks about when I'm with him! It drives me up the wall knowing he's with me but thinking of you! I'm tired of it. Sick of it! I won't put up with your sneaking around to be with him! It was a mean, dirty trick of yours to have that society brat friend of yours set up a phony business date just to get him away from me for a night!"

"That isn't what happened."

"Don't expect me to believe that," Danielle snorted. "They say all's fair in love and war. Well, if you're going to play dirty—I will too!"

Gina listened, stunned, while Danielle ranted on in a tumbling torrent of heated words. Despite her tears, Gina knew that whatever Danielle felt for Jordan—it was not love.

"This is all some kind of mistake," Gina broke in when the fiery girl finally ran down like a wind-up toy. "I don't know what you're talking about or exactly what you're insinuating, but I do know you have some twisted ideas about what's going on. You've seen more of Jordan than I have. I've spent most of my time with Hugh Powers. I think perhaps you should leave now—before we both say things we'll later regret."

Danielle's laugh was brittle. "I'll leave when I'm good and ready and not one moment before. You rich girls make me sick, expecting to dismiss other people from your presence . . . like servants! You've got your money, you've got Hugh. You don't have to snag a rich man like Jordan. You don't need him. Not like *I* do!"

"I don't understand what you mean . . ."

"Of course you wouldn't—you with the silver spoon in your mouth!" Danielle said sarcastically. "Maybe if you'd had my life instead of your own comfortable existence, I

148

wouldn't have to draw you a picture to make you understand. I need Jordan—and I'm going to get him. No one, not you, not anyone, is going to stand in my way. I'll get Jordan Gentry—one way or another—I swear it . . .''

"Does Jordan know all this?" Gina asked.

Danielle gave her a dirty look. "Men are all alike! He'll get what he wants—and give me what I'm after. There's not much time left on this cruise, and I'm not going home without something to show for it! I didn't scrimp and save and carry my lunch in a brown bag every day in order to pay for a luxury cruise, only to have you come along and mess up my plans. No rich society girl is going to upset my applecart. That means you, Gina!"

"Rich? Where do you get the idea I'm rich?" Gina asked. "I happen to work for my living."

"Sure you do! And *I* own the Brooklyn Bridge! Save your cute little story for Hugh, Gina. Do you think people believe that tale about your being a poor working girl? You think you'll find true love if some rich man thinks you're poor? I've got news for you, Gina. You don't fool anyone! Your clothes. Your finishing school accent. Your jewelry. Your luggage. Everything about you reeks of money. Maybe you think Hugh buys that story about your being a poor bookstore clerk, but he knows the truth. You're obviously the type who's gone through life with everything handed to you on a platter. Well, all my life I've had to work to make my own breaks and arrange my own chances! I don't want to work for a pittance forever, wondering how to make ends meet, let alone worrying about how to get ahead. Everyone on the ship knows Hugh Powers is carrying a torch for you and would marry you in a minute. Marry him, Gina, but leave Jordan Gentry for me!"

With that tirade, her eyes brimming with hatred, Danielle shot Gina one more scalding look, then departed in a rapid clack of heels as she stormed from the dining room. Curious diners stared after her and shook their heads with startled sympathy when they smiled at Gina.

Maureen was up when Gina returned to their room.

"You look down in the dumps this morning," she observed.

"So-so," Gina murmured vaguely.

"Wait'll I tell you the news. It's good for a laugh. I almost woke you when I came in last night, but you were sleeping so soundly I didn't have the heart."

"What news? I could use a joke."

"Brent and I were in a disco last night," Maureen explained. "Danielle came in all by herself, looking as if she were searching for someone. Probably Jordan. Anyway, something incredibly funny happened. I pointed her out to Brent—and Gina—he knows her! When Danielle saw Brent, you wouldn't have believed the look on her face. Brent told me she's not the daughter of a wealthy real estate tycoon. She's a teller on vacation from one of their branch banks! I'd never have suspected if Brent hadn't told me. Isn't that the richest thing you've heard all day?"

"Second, perhaps," Gina murmured. "I'm sorry to spoil your news, Maureen, but I already knew about Danielle."

"You knew?" Maureen gasped. "How could you? Who told you?"

"Danielle herself. She cornered me at breakfast and warned me to stay away from Jordan. She told me she hadn't scrimped and saved in order to have me spoil her vacation."

"That explains why she hates you the way she does. She's terrified of losing Jordan as a potential meal ticket."

"That's about it."

"The poor fool," Maureen said. "Danielle probably thinks with all Jordan's money she'd be guaranteed happiness. The truth is, wealth offers its own problems. Danielle will probably have to find out the hard way what any seasoned gold digger could tell her.''

''What's that?''

''That those who marry for money usually earn every dime!''

''If Danielle hadn't told me all this herself, I'd find it hard to believe,'' Gina said. ''She really looked the part she was playing. If she saved every nickel in order to afford the cruise, where did she get the clothes and spending money?''

''The cruise and cash were big items,'' Maureen admitted. ''The clothes? Easy! Danielle probably picked up designer dresses for next to nothing at a charity resale shop. It's possible to find bargains in these shops and dress like a queen for a song.''

Gina nodded. ''Probably. But what about the jewelry?''

''Paste imitations, no doubt,'' Maureen waved her hand. ''The simulated gems are so well-made these days, it's sometimes hard for even a jeweler to tell the genuine from the fake.''

''I'd never thought of that.''

''You wouldn't, Gina. But a hard-nosed, conniving woman like Danielle would. She plays all the angles.''

Gina told Maureen about the scene on the deck the night before. ''As upset as Danielle was, I thought maybe she really cared for Jordan. I was wrong. All she wants is his money.''

''On cruise ships there are a lot of relationships that look like love to the casual eye but are mercenary mergers instead. There are always gold diggers wherever wealthy people gather. After a while most well-heeled people become expert in detecting them. It's one of the tricks that goes with the territory.''

''I feel sorry for Jordan. What if he falls into her trap?''

Maureen laughed. "I doubt that will happen. He's much too astute. I wouldn't be surprised if Jordan doesn't have Danielle all figured out. He won't be her victim. I know he won't."

"How can you be so sure?"

"Because Jordan doesn't love Danielle, Gina. I know that beyond the shadow of a doubt."

"What makes you so certain?"

"Very simple. I know Jordan doesn't love her, **because** it's obvious to Brent and me that Jordan loves *you!*"

With the cruise drawing to an end, Gina grew more and more despondent. She looked forward to the time when she could make arrangements in New York to fly back to the Caribbean to visit Luke. But her heart still ached for the lost relationship with Jordan.

The two days at sea while the *Tropical Star* sailed toward the New York harbor were quiet ones for Gina. She rarely left her stateroom. Jordan never looked her up, and Hugh only rarely sought her out, correctly sensing that she preferred to be left alone. Before Hugh left Gina in peace, he did extract a promise from her to have dinner with him the night they landed in New York.

"When the cruise ends, Gina, I don't want *us* to end."

"It won't be that way," Gina promised. "But I have other things to think about now. There's always the future."

"It's the future I'm counting on," Hugh said softly. "I'm hoping that when we're apart, when you're with your brother, you'll discover that absence makes the heart grow fonder. That you'll realize you love me. I live for the day when you'll be my wife."

"Hugh . . . please!"

"I won't pressure you, Gina. But I will remind you that I want you."

Hugh produced a small business card from his wallet, penned the name of a club and an address on the back of the engraved card, and seemed relieved when Gina promised that even if she saw little—or nothing of him while they sailed for New York, she would be with him the night they landed.

The next day as they drew near to New York City, the ocean air chilled. An atmosphere of excitement pervaded the ship as those who had longed to get away from home now yearned to be back. Maureen bubbled with happy plans for her return to Bridgeton and her reunion with Brent.

Gina anticipated a restful, relaxing, rejuvenating visit with Luke. When Gina questioned Hugh about his plans, he smiled with a distant look and simply shrugged.

The Statue of Liberty beckoning in the harbor brought a lump to Gina's throat. When the liner steamed into its berth and was moored, Gina and Maureen joined the others in disembarking. The customs inspection took longer than Gina expected and she found the wait grueling. To pass the time, she searched the crowd, hoping to catch sight of Jordan. But he was nowhere to be seen.

"Thanks for taking me along, Gina. It's been an unforgettable two weeks. Really wonderful! You're going to have a great time with Luke. I know it. Don't forget to hurry back to us in Bridgeton."

"I was glad to have you with me, Maureen. Don't worry about me. I'll be back in Bridgeton before you have time to realize I'm gone. Tell everyone hello for me."

"Sure thing! Save your first night back in town for Brent and me! We're taking you out to dinner so you can tell us all about your visit with Luke."

A cabbie pulled up and Gina and the driver piled her possessions into the car. Maureen got into another cab and gave Gina an enthusiastic wave before they parted ways.

Gina registered at the hotel, showered, and changed. Almost immediately it was time to summon a taxi to take her to Hugh's club.

Hugh hadn't yet arrived when the cabbie let Gina out in front of a canopied building at the prestigious address. The doorman ushered her into the building. She checked her coat and, when she mentioned Hugh's reservation, the maitre d' nodded and led her to a pleasant table in a secluded section of the room.

Each time a new group of diners entered the room, Gina glanced up, expecting to see Hugh. Each time she was disappointed. The hands of her wrist watch moved slowly. It wasn't like Hugh to be late. Gina began to fear some kind of trouble—a traffic jam, or worse, an accident. A few times her cabbie had taken chances to avoid snarls. Ten minutes later Gina began to worry in earnest.

"Waiting for someone, Gina?"

Gina jumped when a hand touched her bare shoulder. The voice was gentle where once it had held mockery.

Gina stared up, up, into the turquoise eyes of Jordan Gentry.

"As a matter of fact, yes."

"This time you're not waiting for me, either," Jordan said. His eyes crinkled at the corners with amusement.

"No, I'm afraid not," Gina smiled. "Hugh said he'd be meeting me here. I can't imagine what's detained him."

Jordan shrugged. He looked at the vacant chair and asked Gina if she minded if he joined her. He rested his chin on his folded hands and studied Gina intently.

"It was another of Hugh's lies, Gina," Jordan said quietly. "Hugh and I had a little talk when we departed the ship this afternoon. After what I told him about you, I'm afraid he feels he can no longer be bothered with you. I knew his plans, so I made the reservation in Hugh's name,

154

not mine, so the maitre d' would keep you here for me."

"Hugh can't be . . . *bothered?*" The painful words eased past her lips. "What do you mean by that?"

"When I told Hugh you weren't the rich woman he thought you were, I shattered all his plans and dreams. Hugh lost interest in you the moment he discovered you weren't the answer to all his financial problems. You see, Hugh went on the cruise in search of a wealthy woman. He wanted to marry someone who could buy his way out of his problems."

Gina shook her head in amazement. "That can't be true, Jordan. I'm not wealthy and I told Hugh so!"

"You told him, but he chose not to believe you. He thought you were being coy—telling little white lies to protect yourself from . . . exactly his kind—the type of man who marries for money and not for love."

Gina stared at her trembling hands. She fought back the tears of hurt and shock, then asked: "What will happen to Hugh?"

Jordan smiled at the realization that Gina was a woman who would accept hurt from another and then worry about the welfare of the very one who had inflicted the pain.

"God knows. Literally," Jordan said. "It won't be easy for a once wealthy man to adjust to poverty. Hugh is hoping he won't have to. And maybe he won't. The luck of the world seems to be with those who sell their souls and honor. When I left Hugh, he was in Danielle's company—making plans to take her out for a memorable evening." Jordan's voice lowered. "Hugh thinks *Danni* has money!"

Gina gasped at the irony. "But she's not rich. She's only—"

"A bank teller intent on marrying a rich man so she can escape her lot in life."

"Danielle thinks *Hugh* is rich."

Jordan smiled at the thought. "They deserve each other."

"Then you knew about Danielle?"

"That she was after my money?" Jordan answered Gina's question with one of his own. "Yes, I knew. Just as I knew almost from the beginning of the cruise that Hugh was down on his luck and short of cash. All Hugh had left was appearances and a name and reputation that could keep the credit and benefits coming until word spread that he's broke. He is hoping he can marry into money before that day of reckoning arrives. I knew you never loved Hugh, Gina, because you love me. Though God knows I never deserved the love of a woman like you."

"Jordan . . ." Gina breathed his name with disbelief when she understood how much he knew about her.

"During the cruise I did everything possible to kill your love and thwart the feelings I had for you. I managed one way or another to do almost everything imaginable to drive a lovely Christian woman like you away from a man like me. I couldn't succeed in driving you away no matter how much I wanted to avoid you. When I arranged not to see you, someone else managed for us to be thrown together. I couldn't avoid you, couldn't forget you, and couldn't cease loving you because you're the woman God wants for me. When I saw the love in your eyes—love I didn't deserve—I knew it was there not because you wanted it to be there but because God wanted us together."

"I had no idea you knew how I felt," Gina whispered.

"It was meant to be, Gina. And it could have all happened at Christmas except our timing didn't work out. Probably because the Lord knew we weren't ready for each other then. I could have met you at Christmas, but I turned down Luke's invitation to visit him aboard the *Sea Nymph*. Just like you did."

"Luke? You know *Luke?*" Gina cried with surprise.

Jordan grinned and nodded. "I've known Luke for years. I dived from the *Sea Nymph*. Luke and I became like brothers. It was aboard the *Sea Nymph* that I turned my life over to Christ. I turned down Luke's invitation because I didn't want your brother to see me as the man I'd become, Gina. A man who had fallen away from his faith."

Gina was stunned by the knowledge. Then she realized why Jordan had been so sure he knew her. It hadn't been a clever line! It was the truth.

"The name Roberts should've clued me in, but I never gave Luke a thought. Not until that day at the pool when Maureen called you Regina. Suddenly it all clicked into place. I knew I couldn't repay Luke by seducing his sister!"

"That's why you avoided me?"

"I had to. I wanted you, Gina, the way I've never wanted a woman before. It wasn't until much later that I discovered what I felt wasn't lust. It was love—the love I'd been waiting for all my life. The love I was too blind to see until the Lord opened my eyes."

"Jordan . . ." Gina whispered his name and it was like happy music on her lips.

"A man like Luke would want the best for his little sister, Gina. At the time I could see why Luke wanted me to meet his very special sister. But I couldn't understand Luke wanting his sister to meet the likes of me. I haven't been the kind of man Luke remembered in a number of years. Those days are behind me, thank God. With the Lord's help and with renewed faith and a recommitted heart, I know the future will be brighter."

"Hearing you say these things is the answer to one of my most fervent prayers."

"For years I've resisted returning to the ways of God," Jordan continued, "even when He patiently summoned me back from my mistaken path. I wanted the ways of the world. I can no longer face the lonely life I've been living apart from God. I don't want the worldly life. I want serenity. Peace of mind. Happiness. The security only God can give. And I want you, Gina, and the love you have for me. I want you, Regina, the way God intended a man to want a woman when they share their love, their life, and Christ.''

Jordan's strong hand sought Gina's smaller one. She smiled through tears of happiness that filmed her eyes.

"That sounds very much like a marriage proposal, Jordan.''

Jordan's gentle smile warmed Gina's heart. "That's what it is, my darling. Before, I tried to order you to love me. Then, I tried to buy you. Now, in realizing how undeserving I was, I'm asking you to give me your love and accept mine in return. Will you marry me?''

"Knowing everything I know now makes that an easy question to answer. Yes, Jordan. My answer is *yes!''*

"When?'' Jordan whispered the word.

"Today. Tomorrow. Now!'' Gina sighed happily. "Big church. Small one. In a tiny chapel. With all our friends present. Or alone before the Lord. It doesn't matter to me, Jordan, just as long as I can be with you. All my life I've had only one expectation of the man I should marry.''

"And what is that?''

Gina's topaz eyes danced. "I vowed that when I married, Jordan, it would be to a Christian man. In you, my darling, every promise has been fulfilled. And when we say our vows, it will be for the one perfect reason—for love alone.''

MEET THE AUTHOR

SUSAN C. FELDHAKE lives with her husband, Steve, and their children on Sow's Ear Acres, the family farm, in central Illinois. Her interests include canning garden produce, cooking from original recipes, and keeping pioneer arts alive in a modern world. When she isn't working on her novels, Susan likes to read, play the piano, and spend cozy evenings visiting with friends.

Susan came to write this book because a rising divorce rate seemed to indicate that many couples were marrying for short-term and worldly reasons rather than being wed because of enduring spiritual values.

Serenade Books are inspirational romances in contemporary settings, designed to bring you a joyful, heart-lifting reading experience.

Other Serenade books available in your local bookstore:

#1 ON WINGS OF LOVE, Elaine L. Schulte
#2 LOVE'S SWEET PROMISE, Susan C. Feldhake
#3 FOR LOVE ALONE, Susan C. Feldhake
#4 LOVE'S LATE SPRING, Lydia Heermann
#5 IN COMES LOVE, Mab Graff Hoover
#6 FOUNTAIN OF LOVE, Velma S. Daniels and Peggy E. King.

Watch for the Serenade/Saga Series, historical inspirational romances, to be released in January, 1984.